Ben might look like a tough guy on the outside, but he had a sensitive side.

He was sweet. And perceptive. Almost like BJ.

Vee almost choked on her sip of coffee. Ben couldn't possibly be half the man BJ was, nor would he ever be. She jammed that frequency of thinking before it could be broadcast any farther.

Of course she was thankful for Ben's help. He'd been there to rescue her earlier, with his big old tow truck and amiable half grin. And now he was being nice to her father, which was a big plus in her book.

But the feelings she was experiencing—those couldn't be more than mismatched forms of gratitude, could they? She didn't even like Ben.

He might be acting nice today, but not all that long ago he'd broken her best friend's heart.

BJ wasn't like that. That was good enough for her.

Or was it?

Books by Deb Kastner

Love Inspired

A Holiday Prayer
Daddy's Home
Black Hills Bride
The Forgiving Heart
A Daddy at Heart
A Perfect Match
The Christmas Groom
Hart's Harbor
Undercover Blessings
The Heart of a Man

A Wedding in Wyoming
His Texas Bride
The Marine's Baby
A Colorado Match
*Phoebe's Groom
*The Doctor's Secret Son
*The Nanny's Twin Blessings
*Meeting Mr. Right

*Email Order Brides

DEB KASTNER

lives and writes in colorful Colorado with the Front Range of the Rocky Mountains for inspiration. She loves writing for Love Inspired Books, where she can write about her two favorite things—faith and love. Her characters range from upbeat and humorous to (her favorite) dark and broody heroes. Her plots fall anywhere in between, from a playful romp to the deeply emotional. Deb's books have been twice nominated for the *RT Book Reviews* Reviewer's Choice Award for Best Book of the Year for Love Inspired. Deb and her husband share their home with their two youngest daughters. Deb is thrilled about the newest member of the family—her first granddaughter, Isabella. What fun to be a granny! Deb loves to hear from her readers. You can contact her by email at Debwrtr@aol.com, or on her MySpace or Facebook pages.

Meeting Mr. Right

Deb Kastner

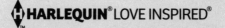

Recycling programs
for this product may
not exist in your area.

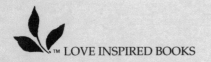 ™ LOVE INSPIRED BOOKS

ISBN-13: 978-0-373-81681-1

MEETING MR. RIGHT

Copyright © 2013 by Debra Kastner

www.LoveInspiredBooks.com

Printed in U.S.A.

You are the light of the world. A city that is set on a hill cannot be hidden. Nor do they light a lamp and put it under a basket, but on a lampstand, and it gives light to all who are in the house. Let your light so shine before men, that they may see your good works and glorify your Father in heaven.

—*Matthew* 5:14–16

To my grandchildren, Izzie and Anthony.
My heart "beeps" for you both.

Chapter One

Dear Veronica Jayne,
I can't believe we have less than two months until our online Spanish class is finished. Have you given any more thought to picking a mission organization? We need to get our applications in soon. I've been seeking the Lord's will on it, but I'll admit I'm dragging my heels a little bit until I know for sure where you are planning to go.

Speaking of our Spanish class, we need to start thinking about how to wrap up our team project. Your idea for our PowerPoint presentation rocks. The Benefits of Knowing Spanish on the Mission Field. It's perfect because we're both going into stateside missions and there are so many Spanish-speaking folks here in America. We'll get an A for our work on the project, and it certainly won't hurt us to

know all about the missions that need our skills
when we're working on our applications.

By the way, what I've seen of the script
you've written is awesome. Keep it up! I'm still
gathering and integrating charts and graphics to go along with the explanations you've
presented.

I've got to say, this collaboration is surprising in more ways than one. I'm so happy that
the professor placed us together as a team.
We work well together. I trust you—especially
because the team project is nearly half of our
grade. Not only that, but I've made a new
friend, which trumps any school grade, even
an A+.

I'm glad that friend is you, Veronica.

Sorry—I'm starting to sound lame. It's late,
and I'd better wrap this up. I have an early day
tomorrow.

All the best,
BJ

*At least I can look forward to working on that
project with BJ,* Veronica Jayne Bishop, known
as "Vee" to everyone in Serendipity, Texas,
thought to herself. *Because the other man I
have to work with today is driving me nuts.*

"I cooked dinner last night." Vee crossed
her arms, leaned her hip against the counter

and glared at the paramedic Ben Atwood, who lounged casually on a folding chair. His legs were stretched out in front of him, crossed at the ankles, and his fingers were laced through the thick ruffle of dark brown hair he wore long enough to curl around his collar.

Their gazes locked. Ben's eyes were arguably his best feature. Displaying both amusement and intelligence, they were a compelling mixture of green and bronze and contained what looked like a purely and disarmingly friendly luminescence that most women would easily get lost in.

But Vee wasn't most women. And she wasn't buying that oh-so-charming demeanor for a moment.

She scoffed inwardly. She knew just exactly what was behind that sparkling gaze, and it didn't bode well for any woman with a lick of sense in her—just ask her dearest friend Olivia Tate, who knew firsthand how unreliable Ben's handsome smile could be. It still rankled Vee every time she thought about it.

"I'm just sayin'—" Ben started to explain, but Vee didn't allow him to finish.

"What? That because I'm a woman, by definition I should do all the cooking at the firehouse? Benjamin Atwood, you know perfectly well that each of us is responsible for one evening a week in front of the hot stove, men and women alike. The fact that I'm the *only* woman who works for this fire department makes your attitude all that much more reprehensible. You're welcome to step into the twenty-first century anytime now."

There was a flash of irritation in his eyes, but it vanished as she watched.

"Okay, first of all, only my mama calls me Benjamin," he drawled, his gaze sparkling as a smile crept up one side of his lips. "And second, that wasn't what I was about to say at all."

He lifted his hands level with his shoulders to show he was harmless. "If you would have let me finish, I would have been able to make my point."

She narrowed her gaze on him suspiciously. "And that would be?"

He chuckled. "Only that I'm the world's worst cook, while the lasagna you made last night was mouth-wateringly delicious." He tilted his head and a shrug rippled across his broad shoulders. "It was supposed to be a compliment."

She arched a brow. His expression was absolutely earnest and without the least bit of guile, so why didn't she believe him?

Let me count the ways, she thought to herself.

Because the man was a chronic liar. And a cheat. He used his charm to get what he wanted.

She couldn't trust him or his winsome smile any further than she could throw him, and because he was a good two-hundred pounds and she a mere one-twenty, that wouldn't be very far.

"No, really," he insisted. "I know it's my turn. Look," he said, swinging off his chair with sleek, catlike grace and reaching for a paper grocery bag on the counter. "See? I came prepared."

Vee peeked skeptically over the rim of the bag. "Cans of chili? What kind of dish are you preparing with that?"

His grin widened. "Chili."

She snorted and shook her head. "Why did I even ask?"

"*Slow cooker* chili," he amended, his brow dancing. "My own secret recipe."

"What makes it a secret?" She had to ask. She really didn't want to make small talk with the man, but she had to admit she was curious.

The bronze in his eyes danced with the green. "If I told you, it wouldn't really be a secret, now would it?"

"Seriously? Do you want me to leave the room while you prepare your *secret* recipe?"

"I'll let you in on it," he acknowledged in a pseudo whisper, "if you promise you won't breathe a word of it to any of the guys."

Vee nodded grudgingly. She didn't like the idea of sharing anything with him—not even a secret—but she couldn't resist a mystery. She watched carefully, curious to see what Ben would add to canned chili to make it his *special recipe,* something her fellow firefighters might find especially unique and tasty.

Vee wondered if Ben's recipe was something his mother had taught him, and then her heart gave a sudden, jagged tug, twisting painfully as she was once again reminded of her own mother's recent passing, just six months ago.

Would it ever get any easier? She would be fine one minute—or at least she'd convince herself she was all right—and then the next she'd be struck by a sharp-toothed edge of grief that made her nearly double over.

"Need help?" she offered, her voice raspy as she fought to control her emotions. She refused to let what she was feeling show on her face. Busy hands and an engaged mind helped her not to dwell on the unpleasant emotions sparring inside her.

"Nope," he replied, turning to plug each of the slow cookers into separate outlets.

Vee stared at his back, letting out her breath when she realized he didn't have a clue that she'd just fought an emotional battle and had barely come out unscathed. This was one time she was thankful for the man's insensitivity.

"As you so enthusiastically reminded me," he continued, tossing a glance over his shoulder, "it's not your day to cook. I've got it covered."

He was right, of course. She *had* just declared that it wasn't her turn to cook. In fact, she'd made a big stink about that very issue. But willingly offering her assistance wasn't the same thing as being expected to do all the work. Besides, it made her antsy to sit around doing nothing.

"At least let me open the cans for you," she insisted, reaching into the paper bag and grasping a can.

He shrugged. "Suit yourself."

She opened several sizeable cans of chili and handed them off to Ben, who scooped the contents into three large olive-green slow cookers that looked like they were throwbacks from the seventies—which they probably were, come to think of it. The men at the firehouse often used the slow cookers to heat their food, allowing them to throw together simple meals that made large portions—the two main requirements in any firehouse kitchen. The boys had hearty appetites, especially after they'd been working out with extra PT—physical training—as they were doing today.

Ben and Vee had been left to cover the firehouse. In case of an emergency, they would be first on call. It was part of their duties as volunteers for the tri-county emergency team. They were each paid a small stipend, but nearly everyone, with the exception of Chief Jenkins, had second jobs to support themselves, Vee included. She worked in the gardening department at Emerson's Hardware. She knew Ben worked at his uncle's auto garage as a mechanic, using the paramedic training he'd learned in the National Guard as a volunteer for the county.

Ben stirred the contents briefly, took a whiff, groaned in anticipation and covered each pot with a glass lid.

Vee raised a brow. "I thought you said you have a special recipe."

"I said I have a *secret* recipe. That's not exactly the same thing."

Vee shook her head. Now she was really confused. "Okay, then…what's the secret? I didn't see you add anything to the beans."

"Exactly." Ben crossed his arms over the broad muscles of his chest, a movement that highlighted his large biceps—which was probably exactly what he'd intended.

Vee remembered him as being rather scrawny and easily overlooked in high school, but he certainly made up for that now. Women flocked to the man like pigeons to a piece of fresh bread. He had the build of a magnificent sculpture, every plane and muscle clearly defined, flaunting the many hours he'd spent in the gym—but sadly enough, he knew it. It was no wonder he drew attention to his physical assets—especially since he so clearly lacked anything emotional or romantic to offer.

"Come again?" she asked, pulling her gaze away from his upper arms.

"I didn't add anything. So you see, that's my *secret*."

Vee didn't want to react. She definitely didn't want to encourage him in any way. But how could she not laugh at the utter ridiculousness of the situation? "So let me get this straight. Everyone else adds herbs and spices to the chili to doctor it up, and you, by contrast, just serve it right out of the can."

His grin widened to epic proportions. He certainly looked pleased with himself. "Brilliant, huh? I'm not too keen on onions and tomatoes, anyway," he informed her, making a face like a five-year-old boy being served brussels sprouts. "Give me good, plain beef steak any day of the week."

"Or chili?"

"Or chili," he agreed with a clipped nod. "I told you I'm a horrible cook. I don't even trust myself to add things to the food that comes out of a can. I wouldn't want to subject anyone else to what qualifies as my attempt to make home-made food from fresh ingredients. No doubt what I'd cook up would be nothing short of a blooming disaster—food so spicy you'd burn your tongue to a crisp and your eyes would water until you couldn't see out of them, or on the flip side, food so bland it'd put you to sleep.

"If it doesn't come out of a can or a bottle, I'm helpless. If I lived in a bigger town I'd order takeout every night. As it is, Cup o' Jo Café and the deli at Sam's Grocery get a lot of my business. I actually enjoy my shifts at the firehouse because I get to eat decently, something a little bit closer to home-cooked."

Vee crinkled her nose. Granted she hadn't been working here very long, but she wouldn't classify any of the food she ate at the firehouse as *decent*. Acceptable at best, and barely palatable at worst. Cans of plain chili might be a promotion from what she was usually subjected to.

"And I visit my mama every Sunday afternoon," he added, more as an exclamation than an afterthought. "She enjoys cooking for her son, and naturally I'm keen to eat whatever she makes for me."

"Spoiled," she quipped, but she nodded in approval just the same. He might be a player with the women he dated, but she knew he took good care of his parents, which Vee had to admit was a small mark in his favor.

Not enough to erase the black smudges, but perhaps a small offset.

"A little," he admitted. "But mostly I'm just being a dutiful son."

"I'm sure your parents appreciate that, especially your mother." Her voice cracked a little on the last word, and she scolded herself for being so transparent in front of him. But she couldn't help remembering how blessed she had felt to have had the chance to spend time with her own family, before her mother's recent passing. Now her dad kept to himself, and neither she nor her two brothers could help him get beyond his grief.

Ben regarded her with a thoughtful frown. "I'm so sorry for your loss. It must be difficult for you, losing your mother."

"What? No. I mean, thank you. At least I know she's with the Lord."

"Yes," he agreed. "Your mom's faith was a real inspiration. But it still must be hard on you, having her pass so suddenly."

She didn't know whether she was more surprised by Ben's openness or the fact that there was a genuine note of compassion in his voice. She knew he was a churchgoing man, but then, so was almost every man in Serendipity. Attending church didn't necessarily mean he was a man of faith.

"It was difficult to lose her," she admitted, wondering how they'd gotten on such a serious topic—how he'd turned the conversation and gotten her to talk about herself. She didn't know why she continued, but she did. "It's still difficult. To be honest with you, I don't quite know how to respond when someone says they feel sorry for me."

She shrugged away the statement, wishing it could be simple to shirk off the turmoil of emotion teetering near the edge of her consciousness. She didn't like feeling as if she were on the verge of an emotional breakdown all the time. She preferred to keep her feelings locked tightly away.

"It's a good thing that you're close to your family. There's nothing wrong with that. And despite my loss, I'm still blessed to have my father and brothers, although we don't get together as often as I'd like now that we're all grown up and living away from home."

"Right. There's a change in family dynamics when we reach adulthood. How does Cole like the Navy?"

"Are you kidding? He was born for service," she said, cheering up a little at the change of topic. Cole was the middle of the three Bishop children, the one who was always causing mischief of one sort or another—often involving his naive little sister and leading her into trouble. Now those days seemed pleasantly nostalgic.

"Cole was always one of the tough guys, and serving the country in the military suits him. Same with Eli. He was playing cops and robbers from the time he could walk," she commented of her oldest brother. "I guess it's lucky for us he ended up on the *cop* side of the equation."

Ben chuckled at her weak attempt at humor. "And you, the firefighter."

"Me, the firefighter," she agreed. "But I never played with matches. No correlation there."

"Never?" he asked, a curious gleam in his eye. "Come on. You can admit it. I won't tell."

She gnawed thoughtfully on her bottom lip, wondering how much she should divulge. Was he baiting her, or was this a sincere attempt on his part to be civil? She decided to take a chance on him. A very *small* chance. "I might have lit a twig on fire…once or twice, when I was little."

One side of his mouth crept upward in an appealing half smile, the one that sent the single female population of Serendipity all aflutter.

"Now we're getting to the good stuff. If the fellows here at the firehouse ever learned that you—"

"But you said—"

Jerk.

"Your secret is safe with me," he assured her. "I'm just teasing. I won't say anything. Besides, if that's the worst of your record, I can assure you that you're lagging far behind me."

"Is that right? How so?"

He returned to his folding chair and leaned his elbows against the long table. His gaze met and locked with hers. "We all have some skeletons in our closets, don't you think? I'm every bit as human as the next guy."

"Really?" Was he sorry for the mistakes he'd made, the way he'd hurt people like Olivia? As far as she knew, he'd never apologized. And even if he had, he'd done some truly callous things in his past, things Vee was slow to forgive.

"I'm just saying my secrets are probably, shall we say, more *interesting* than yours?"

If he thought of his secrets as "skeletons in the closet" then they were probably nothing she would want to know. Her own best, most closely held secret was light and bright and made her grin every time she thought of it. In this case, she highly doubted that any one of his secrets could rival hers. She smothered her grin behind her fist.

Lighting a few pine twigs on fire with a magnifying glass in the sunshine didn't even begin to cover the mysteries she was hiding in her heart. Her mind immediately flashed to the wonderful internet relationship she was building with BJ. She'd met him through a college-level online Spanish class. They'd been paired up together for a project and had been emailing each other daily for the several weeks since. She'd started anticipating his emails, and reading them had become the best part of her day.

That she'd never seen him in person was just a trivial detail. They weren't officially dating or anything—it wasn't probable that she could form a truly romantic relationship in cyberspace—but they'd often spoken of working at the same mission, more and more as the days went by—and who knew what would happen then?

BJ definitely qualified as a *secret*. She hadn't told a single soul in Serendipity about him, not even her best friend, Olivia. It might be pride, or even embarrassment at the fact that the closest thing she had to a real relationship was a cyber Prince Charming, but right now, this minute, BJ was hers and hers alone. Her heart warmed just thinking about him.

She realized Ben was staring at her speculatively and a blush rose to her face. It was disconcerting to realize his gaze could affect her, even if what she was feeling was discomfiture.

"You look like you're deep in thought," he teased. "Anything else you want to 'fess up to?"

Like she'd tell him.

She tossed her chin and scoffed dramatically. "Wouldn't you like to know."

"You'd better believe it," he agreed, his grin deepening to reveal his dimples. His eyes sparkled.

She took a deep breath, mentally coaching herself to relax her shoulders. The warmth spreading from her chest to her face had nothing to do with Ben, she assured herself, but it still disquieted her.

Ben was a flesh-and-blood man sitting directly opposite her. She could reach out and touch him if she wanted to—and that was the problem. Even if Ben hadn't been someone she disliked on principle, teasing and flirting just weren't her style. She knew that had to be the reason why she'd gotten through so many years without a serious relationship.

But online was a completely different story. BJ was safe because he wasn't entirely real, so she didn't have to be nervous when they chatted. She could share her enthusiasms and talk freely with him, sometimes even flirt a little. As a result, she felt closer to him than to most of the people in town she'd known all her life. People like Ben Atwood.

She may not have met BJ in person, but she knew he was kind and thoughtful with a heart driven toward helping others. She didn't have to see him face-to-face to know all of that.

She also could see exactly the kind of man Ben was. He was right before her eyes.

A heartbreaker.

Chapter Two

Dear BJ,

I'm still working on the script for our project. I haven't had time this week to do much more than try to keep up on the reading assignments, much less work on the draft. It's that time of year again. My schedule is filled to the brim with flowers, flowers, flowers.

I love planting seeds in the springtime. Winter has borne down upon the land, harsh and unforgiving, but seeds hold the fresh promise of spring inside them. It's humbling to hold such future magnificence in the palm of my hand. And then to clip the blooms and arrange them into beautiful bouquets—could there be anything lovelier?

On another topic, what are your thoughts about the Sacred Heart Mission to America? I've been researching them and I've learned that they're usually right in the middle of the action, building shelters and offering both physical and spiritual aid for folks affected by hurricanes, tornadoes or floods.

I don't know about you, but that's what I'm looking for—to be where people need me. I can't imagine anything better than to minister to others during their hardest struggles, and I know you share the dream. I'm sure your skills in the medical field will be highly valued.

I'm anxious to hear your thoughts—school wise, mission wise, and anything else you care to add.

Faithfully waiting,

Veronica Jayne

Ben snapped his laptop closed and grinned. He could always count on an email from Veronica Jayne to have him smiling from ear to ear. Beautiful Veronica Jayne, his refined, gracious flower girl, his very own My Fair Lady. Even her name was feminine and graceful. He didn't have to see a picture of her to know she was exquisite. Her elegance shined through every word she wrote. In a word, she simply charmed him.

He'd finished his morning workout early in his rush to get home and see if Veronica Jayne had replied to his email, so he decided to use his extra time to walk over to his folks' house to see how they were faring. He'd missed the previous weekend's Sunday dinner because of an emergency call. Though his parents were in perfect health, they were getting up in years and Ben still worried, despite their protests. He wanted to make sure everything was going well—and maybe catch a bite to eat, if he timed it just right.

As he strode the short distance to his parents' residence, he mused about last night, when he'd been kicking back with Vee Bishop at the firehouse. He was surprised at how much she'd had to say to him—usually she went out of her way to keep her distance. But last night, she'd opened up—just a little. Her cryptic response to his question about what secrets she wasn't revealing intrigued him, even knowing it was none of his business whatsoever.

Frankly, he was surprised she hadn't told him so herself.

When he'd started mindlessly carrying on about the theme of secrets, he'd half expected her to blow him off completely. That or blow *up* at him. He was fairly certain she didn't particularly like him, although exactly why that was he couldn't say. She'd been short with him on more than one occasion in the past.

But in this instance, she *hadn't* blown him

off, nor had she become angry. Instead, she'd
gracefully sidestepped the whole subject, which
intrigued him far more than if she'd become
annoyed. What she did or did not care to share
with him was none of his business. They might
have lived in the same town all their lives, but
in truth they didn't even know each other particularly well.

While he was fairly certain he'd rattled her
with his tactless digging, for once he seemed to
have avoided making her angry. He wished he
knew how he'd dodged the bullet this time—
usually it seemed like everything he did upset
or offended her, even if she rarely vented her
feelings out loud.

He increased his pace as a shiver ran through
him. He'd be the first to admit he had trouble speaking to women. They were a complete
enigma to him in every way, and he put his boot
in his mouth more often than not. His appalling trail of failures with the list of women he'd
dated proved that point in a major way.

The only consolation was that his very clue-
lessness usually convinced his ex-girlfriends
that he hadn't meant any harm. In most cases,
he'd been able to charm his way back into being
friends. But any attempt to charm Vee only
seemed to make her angrier.

Vee was a tough nut to crack. She intimidated him with the way she pulled her hair back into a stark bun that defined her cheek-bones into sharp lines, not to mention the incessant way she was always scowling at him with a permanent frown etched into her features whenever he was around. That he'd gotten her to laugh once or twice during their exchange the night before was definitely the exception to the rule. Maybe he was making some progress.

"Progress" just made him think of the other projects in his life—like his plans for mission work, for example, and the online Spanish class he was taking to prepare.

But most of all, he thought about the plans to meet and hopefully date his beautiful Veronica Jayne.

No one in Serendipity knew of the developing relationship with his internet classmate. Not his paramedic partner Zach Bowden. Not his friends. Not even his parents. He supposed that deep down he just wasn't ready to share her yet.

What a sweet secret to have.

Ben grinned to himself as he reached the one and only intersection off of Main Street, glanced both ways and crossed over to the other side. Serendipity, with its population of less than a thousand, didn't even merit a stop-light and just barely bothered with three-way stop signs. There was seldom traffic to watch out for, and today was no exception.

In fact, it was an unremarkably quiet day in Serendipity, with most folks going about their business as usual. Even the three retired men in their matching bib overalls who usually congregated in front of Emerson's Hardware in their wooden rocking chairs were nowhere to be seen.

With nothing interesting to view on the horizon, Ben's mind shifted to Veronica Jayne and the unlikely development of their cyber relationship. It had started innocently enough, emailing each other back and forth about their combined class project. After a while the conversation had drifted to chattering about weekly assignments, and before he knew it, they were talking personal issues—sometimes *very* personal issues, especially when they'd discovered they had the same plans for stateside mission work.

He'd been praying for his future wife for some time now, and if he was being honest with himself, the thought that Veronica Jayne might be *that* woman had crossed his mind more than once, even if they'd agreed they wouldn't pursue anything romantic until—and if—they met in person.

Frankly, it was easier keeping Veronica Jayne

at a distance, on the other end of cyberspace, where he wasn't as apt to screw things up. He didn't exactly have a stellar track record where women were concerned.

He'd been a skinny, awkward teenager who was often embarrassed and humiliated by school bullies, a boy who hid in his uncle's auto garage to avoid having to deal with his callous peers, never mind girls his age, who would either ridicule or ignore him. Girls simply weren't interested in boys like him. His mother had told him not to worry, that his day would come, but he hadn't believed her.

Then, in a desperate attempt to get away from everything and everyone he knew, he'd enlisted in the Army National Guard Reserves. He'd bulked up and put on a uniform, and that had changed *everything*. He'd returned to Serendipity to find the women—those same girls who'd thumbed their noses at him in his youth—all grown up and fawning over him.

He was the first to admit he hadn't handled it very well. What could he say? He was a guy, and the attention of pretty ladies went straight to his head. Being as inexperienced as he was in the world of women, he knew he'd made quite a few mistakes along the way.

How was he supposed to know that after two or three dates, a girl would assume that they were dating exclusively and that he wasn't seeing anyone else? He hadn't even been looking for a serious relationship—not then, anyway—despite the impression he'd apparently given. He'd quickly learned that women had certain ideas in their heads, and they weren't very forgiving when he didn't catch their unspoken implications.

Which he rarely did. He didn't know how to guess how a woman thought. He hadn't known then, and he certainly didn't know now.

No, he'd had enough of all that, thank you very much. Perhaps that was why the idea of finding someone *outside* Serendipity sounded so appealing to him. Someone who didn't know what he'd been like as a kid. Someone unaware of his recent screw-ups in the love department.

If he left Serendipity, he could reinvent himself into anything he wanted to be. A tough guy or a dashing charmer. Sensitive or daring. It was a heady notion. But there was more to it than that. He truly felt called to make a difference on a scale he could never achieve in his small hometown. He wanted to get involved in difficult and often perilous stateside mission work, perfect for an adrenaline junkie like him who wanted to be part of an organization that ministered to people, body and soul.

At times he even dared to imagine the possibility of having a classy, incredible woman working at his side—a strong, independent, caring, Christian woman ready and able to both handle the worst and pray for the best.

It wasn't completely beyond the realm of possibility that this woman was Veronica Jayne. In their emails, her dreams and future plans and goals matched his, and their personalities melded perfectly, each playing off the other's strengths.

But that was online.

Reality? Well, that was probably nothing more than empty space. Would he even know her if he passed by her on the street? Would they connect on that kind of level?

He was almost certainly grasping at straws. If anything ever *did* happen between them, and that was a big *if,* Veronica Jayne eventually would learn everything about him—including his past, which he was still ashamed to think about. Then there was the fact that he had perpetual grease under his nails from working as a mechanic. And the fact that he lived in a miniscule Texas town—he had the impression, though she'd never stated outright, that she lived in a big city.

If he took her home, his mother would no doubt bring out his baby pictures and his yearbook, which would only serve to further humiliate him. One look and Veronica Jayne would discover what a gawky, pimple-covered youth he'd been. Too tall for his skinny physique and all elbows and knees.

He wasn't sure he was ready for that. Anyway, he was getting way ahead of himself. They'd never met in person. Who knew if they'd even like each other when that time came, much less in any kind of romantic capacity? He must be getting soft in the head.

The moment he rounded the corner onto his parents' cul-de-sac, he noticed the black truck parked in his parents' driveway. The back end was loaded with red bricks and multi-colored rocks of various shapes and sizes and bags upon bags of soil and fertilizer. It wasn't an old truck, but it wasn't a new one either. It had some wear—definitely a sensible working vehicle. And though it looked vaguely familiar, he couldn't immediately put a name to the owner. He was fairly certain he hadn't serviced it at the auto shop recently, yet he could picture the vehicle in his mind, sans contents. So where did he know it from?

One way to find out.

He heard someone singing before he even reached the front porch. More telling, it was a *female* singing, or humming rather, and it definitely wasn't his good, old-fashioned country mother, unless she'd developed a sudden propensity for something that sounded suspiciously like classical music to Ben's untrained ears.

Instead of approaching the front door, his curiosity led him around the side of the house to see whose pretty, richly husky alto laced the air with Beethoven, or Bach or whatever it was.

When he got his first glance of her, he nearly stumbled with surprise.

Vee Bishop.

What was she doing here? She hadn't mentioned visiting his parents when they'd been talking the prior evening.

She had her back to him, her slender figure accentuated as she stood on tiptoe on the top rung of a stepladder, precariously reaching for a flowerpot that dangled just out of her reach on a hook next to the patio door. She thought she was alone, as evidenced by the fact that she was humming aloud to the tune of the small mp3 player she had clipped to her belt.

"Beethoven?" he called. With his mind busy creating and discarding reasons why Vee might be in his parents' backyard, he realized only *after* he'd spoken that she couldn't have seen him approach and that the sound of his voice might startle her. She'd managed to unhook the basket with the tips of her fingers, but she didn't have the basket firmly in her grasp and she overreached her mark at the sound of his voice. Wavering in a futile attempt to balance herself, she put one hand out to grasp for the wall, but nothing was there to stop her from falling backward. She squeaked in dismay, and her arms flailed wildly as she attempted to right herself against the ladder.

Ben acted instinctively, darting forward to sweep Vee into his arms before she hit the pavement. He barely felt the weight of her frame as he protectively flexed his biceps to curl her into the safety of his embrace, but he was intensely aware of the moment she wrapped her arm around his neck. The hook of the hanging basket she'd managed to hold on to dug deeply into his shoulder. The sensation didn't register as pain, maybe because his adrenaline was so high. Her free palm rested against his chest, directly over his rapidly beating heart. He wondered if she could feel the pounding staccato rhythm of his pulse.

Crazy woman. What had she been thinking? It was a good thing for her that he'd arrived when he did. He hoped she realized that he had barely averted a disaster.

She could have had broken bones. Been knocked unconscious. Suffered a concussion. He could easily tick a dozen frightening scenarios off on his fingers.

He didn't immediately release her, giving them both time to get their bearings. For a moment she just stared up at him, her cheeks flushed a pretty crimson. Her dark eyes first flared with surprise and then simply sparkled with what Ben suspected was mirth, though he couldn't imagine what she considered to be funny in this situation.

"Mozart," she informed him, wriggling out of his grasp as if she only now realized that he was still holding her up. She stood to her full height, but even so, the top of her head didn't reach Ben's shoulder. "And you should be ashamed of yourself, sneaking up on a person that way. You nearly scared the life out of me. I could have really been hurt there!"

"I didn't sneak," he responded, trying to keep his jaw from dropping. Why was *she* chewing *him* out? She should be eternally grateful for his efforts on her behalf. "What I *did* was save you from a major catastrophe just now. You should be thanking me, not railing on me. And you should know better than to stand on the top rung of a ladder. It's dangerous."

"It's just a step stool," she rejoined with a scowl. Now *that* was a familiar expression from her, especially combined with her backing away from where his outreached hand tried to offer her some support. Although she'd landed in his arms and had not—thanks to him—taken a digger on the ground, she brushed off her jeans as if she'd hit the dirt on both knees.

"Maybe," he conceded. "But you're still begging for an accident by name. In case you're not aware of the rules, you're not supposed to stand on the very top rung of a ladder, step stool or otherwise. You can't balance that way. Didn't anyone ever teach you better?" He kept his tone light and hoped his words sounded like banter and not a reprimand.

It partially worked. Her frown eased a little, though it didn't go away. She rolled her eyes and took another step back. "Are you kidding? With an overprotective dad and two big brothers, I've had every lecture in the book and then some."

"Any reason why this lesson didn't stick?"

She tilted her head thoughtfully and shrugged. "Sometimes they do, sometimes they don't. I'm pretty independent. I've been told I'm stubborn, too, if my brothers have an opinion about it."

Her response seemed serious, and she was still frowning at him. Ben wasn't sure what to say or why the woman was so determined to be angry with him when he'd just saved her from breaking her neck.

He shifted from foot to foot, measuring his words before speaking to the overly testy woman. Speaking suddenly felt like a new and difficult skill, one of which he was nearly incapable. He hadn't yet sorted out words in his brain, much less found the faculties necessary to utter them from his lips, before she spoke again.

"Climbing to the top rungs of ladders is just one of many of the perils of being short," Vee explained. She waved the hanging basket in front of him. "At least I got the basket, thank you very much."

"Right," he agreed, but he was shaking his head. "We wouldn't want you to have to climb back up on that ladder and risk putting life and limb in danger again." He paused and cocked his head, staring at her speculatively. "So tell me why, exactly, are you stealing flowerpots from my parents' backyard?"

Her frown deepened, and for a moment he worried that she'd taken his teasing seriously. She was always pretty quick to think the worst of him. To his relief, she relaxed after a moment instead. "Of course I'm not trying to steal anything. Your folks asked me to come here to do a little spring landscaping for them."

"Why would they do that? If they want some work done, I can do it for them."

That, and the fact that of all the people on the planet they'd chosen to work on their yard, it had to be the one woman he had trouble working with at all. And he *would* be working here, now that he'd discovered his parents' plan. But there was no reason why Vee had to stay. All he had to do was to talk his parents out of this decision, which shouldn't be that difficult, right? Then Vee could go on her merry way.

Her eyes widened and she stared at him like he was slow on the uptake. Could she really blame him? He was still reeling from the nearly averted disaster of catching a plunging-to-the-pavement woman. His heart was still pounding heavily in his chest, stoked by adrenaline. He couldn't set it aside as easily as she appeared to have done.

"It's my job, remember?" she pointed out in a pithy tone of voice. "I work at Emerson's Hardware. Lawn and garden. Ring a bell? I know I've waited on you at least a few times over the years."

"No, of course I know you work at Emerson's," he said, quickly backtracking. Was she making fun of him? "What I meant was, why are you *here,* in my parents' backyard, trying to release flowerpots from their hooks? They didn't mention any gardening projects. I'm surprised they didn't consult me first."

"Why would they?"

Ouch. She had a point, and she hadn't made it softly, either.

His parents didn't need *his* permission to landscape their yard, but it disturbed him just the same that they hadn't asked for his help. He was more than willing to lend a hand. And seriously, what could Vee do for them that he couldn't do himself?

"I can dig in the dirt as well as anyone. For *free*," he added with extra emphasis. His parents were paying good money when they didn't need to be.

Her dark eyebrows rose in perfect curves. "I'm a landscaping specialist, you know. There's a lot more to it than just digging in the dirt. Apparently your parents seem to think I'm needed here."

"Apparently," he repeated, absently rubbing a spot on his temple that was beginning to throb incessantly. He didn't get many headaches, but he had a feeling that today might be the exception.

"You don't believe me?" She gestured toward the sliding glass door that led to the dining room of the Atwoods' house. "Be my guest. Ask your mom why she hired me."

It wasn't that he thought she was lying when she'd stated that his parents had hired her. He just didn't want to accept it. The real problem here, as he was well aware, was that his pride was wounded. He knew it shouldn't matter that they'd hired, of all people, Vee to do their yard work, but that knowledge scraped across every self-righteous nerve in his body.

Did his parents think he wasn't up to a simple landscaping job? Did they think Vee could do it better?

Honestly. How hard could it be to plant a few flowers and trim a few shrubs? They could have at least asked him if he wanted to do it before they called on outside help. He was certain he could do at least as good a job as Vee.

"If you'll excuse me, I'll be back in a moment," he said, gesturing to the back door. "I want to speak with my mom for a second."

"Sure," she agreed. "I'll be here, planting my flowers and humming my Mozart."

"You do that. And try not to fall off any step stools while I'm gone."

"I'll keep that in mind."

As Ben entered the house through the sliding glass door, familiar sights and smells enveloped him. He breathed deeply and released the tension corded through his neck and shoulders. It was amazing how comforting it was simply to step into the house where he'd spent his youth. Entering his home was like being wrapped in a cozy blanket, not only for warmth but for reassurance.

"Mom?" he called as he wiped his feet on the welcome mat by the door. "It's Ben. Where are you?"

"In the kitchen, honey."

He should have known that's where she would be. His mother was always in the kitchen, baking things from scratch. Cooking was her hobby, and she was excellent at it. She spent hours every week poring over cookbooks and magazines trying to find new dishes to try or new twists on old favorites. It wasn't until Ben was an adult that he'd really learned to appreciate the work she did.

He inhaled deeply and groaned with pleasure. The whole house smelled like cinnamon and fresh bread. If he was lucky, she was baking his favorite rolls. His mouth was watering already.

"What's wrong?" she asked as he entered and before he'd said so much as a single word. His mother was like that—naturally intuitive where her children were concerned. So why hadn't she realized he'd be bothered by her landscaping plans?

"I saw Vee outside," he said, trying for a conversational tone, though he doubted he succeeded.

"Oh, yes. Isn't she a dear, willing to work on

our yard even when it's nippy outside? She said she likes being outside, whatever the weather. I really like her. Smart and sensible. And she's a cute little thing, too, don't you think?"

Ben's gaze widened. Whatever else he thought of Vee, he'd never categorize her as a *cute little thing.* Fearless, maybe. Spirited, definitely. But cute?

Not only that, but if he wasn't mistaken, it sounded like his mother was hinting at something beyond simply drawing his attention to the fine work Vee was doing. His mother had been trying to set him up with women since the day he turned twenty. Apparently she wanted grandchildren, and the sooner the better.

But Vee? That was definitely pushing the limits, even for his mother. Vee had never made any secret of the fact that she didn't care for him, and someone as perceptive as his mother had to have noticed.

As if to make it up to him for the suggestion, she pushed a dessert plate loaded with freshly baked cinnamon rolls in his direction. He poured himself a tall glass of milk and settled down with his favorite treat. At least he had timed *that* right.

"Are you having trouble with your yard?" he queried before popping a large chunk of cinnamon roll in his mouth. "Why didn't you come to me for help? I would have been happy to have done your project for you."

His mother's gaze widened in surprise at the change of subject and then narrowed on Ben. "I see," she murmured, not taking her eyes off of him.

He sunk a little lower in his chair at the maternal look she was giving him. It was *the look,* the one that brought down many a child. Ben might be a full-grown man, but it still affected him.

"I'm just asking."

His mother nodded thoughtfully. "Do you have training in landscape architecture?" She paused for less than one second. "No? I didn't think so. That's why I hired Vee," she explained smoothly, wiping her hands on the frilly green apron tied at her waist.

"Did you see the pretty tulips and daffodils already blooming out front next to the dogwood tree?" she continued. "That's Vee's work. She planted a few bulbs for us last fall. It made such a difference in the front that when spring arrived, we decided to hire her to rework our backyard, too. I'm very excited to make more changes in our yard. Your father and I have been talking about doing it for years, but it never seemed like quite the right time. I'm finally going to have the garden I've always wanted."

"I'm as good with a shovel as anyone," he insisted. "Surely I can plant your seeds and tend to your flowers for you. I'm happy to help. You don't need to pay anybody."

"I think I do. It's more than just planting and watering—Vee is designing it all to look just right. I've seen some of the work she's done for our neighbors and I love it. Plus, she has the know-how to pick the right plants to match the weather and amount of shade, to make it all as little work for me to maintain as possible. And that's just the flowers. She has equally wonderful ideas for the vegetable garden. This is how I want to spend my money, Ben. I want everything perfect so your father and I can relax and enjoy ourselves in the backyard. Vee has all kinds of lovely ideas for the backyard and the garden." His mother's face brightened and she slapped both hands on the counter in her exuberance. She was apparently really excited for this garden of hers.

"But if you're eager to help, then that's wonderful," his mother exclaimed. "I may even ask you to build me a gazebo after all the landscaping is finished and my garden is planted. And I'm sure Vee can use you today, too. Most certainly you can do the grunt work—digging in the dirt, like you said. You did enough of that as a young boy. I'm sure you're an expert by now.

That will give Vee more time to focus on the brainwork and not have to get her lovely hands so dirty. Bless you, sweetheart, for offering to help."

He hadn't exactly offered, but what else could he say when his mother leaned across the counter and kissed his cheek with unbridled enthusiasm? He didn't want to let her down, especially since he'd run off at the mouth so much today already.

She knew exactly what she was doing, too—forcing him into this situation, knowing perfectly well that he could not and would not turn her down.

Oh, well. A little dirt never hurt anyone, right? Working with Vee, though? That might be another thing entirely.

Chapter Three

Dear Veronica Jayne,
You know why you're so special? You challenge me to look at the world around me through new eyes. To me, planting anything is just—well—digging in the dirt.

I tend to see life around me that way, too—in black-and-white. It's only since I've been writing to you that I've started to see colors blooming in my world. You're my flower girl.
All the best,
BJ

"Did you get everything straightened out with your mom?" Vee asked as Ben returned to the back patio. Not that she really had to ask to know how the conversation had gone. Even with only a sidelong glance, she could see that his face was the color of a ripe cherry.

"If by 'straightened out' you mean my mother set me in my place and told me to keep my mouth shut and help you dig, then yes. I've definitely been straightened out."

"I didn't mean to cause any problems for you, Ben."

He arched a brow as if he doubted her good intentions. "No, of course you didn't. It's my own blustering that got me into trouble. I may be a thirty-year-old man, but Mama won't take any sass from me."

Vee's throat burned and she quickly turned her gaze from his, blinking rapidly as memories of her own mother overwhelmed her again.

The recollections made her want to laugh.

And cry.

Maybe both simultaneously.

She pulled in a ragged breath, but the air seemed sharp, piercing her throat and lungs. Not a day went by that she didn't think about her mother. She'd be all right for a while, and she even felt like she could function normally most days, but then grief would sneak up and reappear out of nowhere, jumping out from behind her back and wrenching her heart in two once again.

This was one of those times, and she was mortified that Ben was here to witness it once more. Dealt with the sudden blow of emotions she was unable to handle, she would have turned away to hide them, but Ben gently stayed her with his large, calloused hand as he grasped her elbow.

"I did it again, didn't I?" he murmured in an unexpectedly tender, soft tone. "I have a bad habit of sticking my boot in my mouth." Ben was a rough-edged man, and in Vee's opinion, not a very nice one, so the sympathy pouring from his gaze surprised her. "I'm truly sorry about your mother, Vee."

He didn't say anything else. In her experience, people tended to chatter when they were uncomfortable with a situation, but not Ben. He just stood there, strong and silent, waiting for her to gather herself together. She wasn't sure how he'd figured out where her thoughts had gone, but she was grateful to him for giving her the moment she needed to compose herself.

But composure failed to come. Despite her best intentions, tears welled. She fought and nearly lost herself to the blaze that was burning in her throat and behind her eyes.

She wasn't a bawler. She'd learned long ago that crying didn't get you anywhere—not with two big brothers around to tease her about it. If anything, breaking into tears only made things worse, so she'd learned not to do it. Her brothers had literally thrown her into the deep end of the pool and expected her to swim. They'd taught her to be tough. She was a Bishop, and Bishops were a strong lot.

But in this case, reminding herself of her heritage didn't seem to help. Nothing did. She wasn't sure if she could keep her tears from falling despite her best efforts.

Ben slipped his arm around her shoulder and pulled her into a close embrace. The comfort of his rock-solid chest and the steady sound of his heartbeat somehow reassured her.

Depending on someone else, even for a moment, was unfamiliar to her. And she couldn't believe that the person she was leaning on was Ben Atwood—possibly the least reliable person she knew. She squeezed her eyes closed and tried to breathe slowly, fighting desperately against the urge to let loose the roaring broil of her emotions and bawl into Ben's chest. She barely restrained herself from wrapping her arms around his waist and hugging him back.

She couldn't break down. Not here. Not now. Not in front of Ben. Bishops were strong people, she reminded herself again. They didn't let anything get the best of them, not even a grief that felt like it was ripping her apart.

She sucked in another big gulp of air and backed away. The sudden sensation of warm fur crisscrossing her ankles in a figure eight caused her to jolt, but she was careful not to step on whatever it was that was twirling around at her feet. She looked down to find a large gray poof-ball rubbing against her and purring louder than the engine on her truck.

"Is that a cat?" she asked with a chuckle that came out as half a sob. She hitched her breath.

Ben leaned down and scooped the ball of fur into his arms, brushing the hair back from the feline's face with the palm of his hand. Vee could barely make out eyes and a black button of a nose.

"This," Ben said, "is Tinker. And you should feel privileged. He's given you quite an honor. He doesn't usually take to people he doesn't know very well."

As he said the words, the cat sprung from his arms to hers. She caught him with an exclamation of surprise.

"Warn me, next time, will you, kitty?" She tucked Tinker under her chin, oddly comforted by the vibration of the cat's purr and the warmth of his fur.

"I never had a kitten," she said, stroking Tinker's soft, downy fur. "Or a dog. My mom was one of those people who thought all animals should stay outside in the barn."

Another hiccup.

Ben jammed his hands into the front pockets

of his jeans and rocked back on his heels, not speaking but urging her on with a smile.

"I had a hamster once, though, when I was about nine. Alvin the hamster. He'd run on his little wheel all night long. That sound was like a lullaby to me. I slept so soundly when he was around."

"Tinker is a second-generation Atwood cat," Ben explained, reaching out to tickle Tinker under his chin. "His mama was Belle. Tinkerbelle, actually, but most of the time I just called her Belle."

"Oh, my," exclaimed Vee, putting two and two together. "Please don't tell me that this poor boy…"

"…is Tinkerbelle the Second. In my defense, I was a teenager at the time, and kittens weren't a big deal to me. I was too busy worrying about my social life, which…well…" He cut himself off and gave her a charming smile. She noticed it looked a little strained around the edges, as if he disliked thinking back on those memories but was trying to hide it. "I gave him his moniker without actually bothering to see if it was a he or she, and my mother didn't correct me. I think maybe she was trying to teach me a life lesson. Tinker here got the bad end of that deal."

"Poor Tinker," Vee said on a long, counterfeit sigh, stroking the cat from the top of his head to the tip of his tail, causing his purr to rumble even louder. "It's a wonder he still associates with you at all."

"Yeah," Ben agreed with a self-deprecating shrug. "You're probably right about that."

Tinker started wiggling, and Vee reluctantly released him to the ground. "I think Tinker is giving me a nudge. I suppose I've had enough of a work break now. Your parents aren't paying me to talk. I should get back to planting flowers."

She turned, then paused, her shoulders tensing as she realized she'd returned to a touchy subject for Ben. Was he going to belittle her efforts again—tell her once more how little he valued all her careful planning and design work? She shouldn't have been surprised that he had no appreciation for her craft, yet she had still felt hurt at his clear dismissal earlier.

"Where would you like me to start digging?" Ben asked, surprising her when he reached for a nearby shovel.

Vee released a quiet breath. Gardening was her comfort zone, her sweet spot where she could let go of everything else and just be thankful to God for His beautiful creation. Some might see it as just "digging in the dirt," but for her, working with flowers brought Vee her greatest joy.

Did she want to share that with Ben?

Not really. But if putting him to work meant he'd stop giving his mother a hard time, then what choice did she have? Maybe if he could see how dedicated she was to the task, he'd realize that her work truly was important—to her, if not to him.

She pointed to the flower beds on opposite sides of the screened-in back fence, and then at the large plot she'd lined out with stakes and thread marking a place for the garden.

"If you'd please break up and turn the earth for me, I'd appreciate it. I'll bring you a bag of compost so you can fertilize as you go."

"I'll get it," he offered. "It's in the back of your truck, right?"

"Yes, it is." She hesitated. "I hate to have you make two trips, but can you also bring back some potting soil for me? I brought new annuals, mostly petunias and mums, to plant in the hanging pots."

Ben assented with a nod and strode away. Vee's gaze followed him until he turned the corner of the house. Then she propped her hands on her hips and surveyed the property, ticking off projects in her mind. The flower beds would be the home to a dozen new rosebushes, and the garden still needed to be seeded with vegetables. Several decorative pots for the back porch awaited her attention, too.

Now, where had she been before Ben arrived?

Oh, right. The hanging basket. Falling into Ben's arms. How could she have forgotten that so easily? It was not her most graceful moment. Her face flamed just thinking about it, so she redirected her thoughts to the tasks at hand.

She was gathering a variety of hanging and standing flowerpots into a line on the porch when Ben returned to the backyard, a twenty-five-pound bag of potting soil under one arm and a fifty-pound bag of fertilizer slung over his other shoulder. She hadn't expected him to bring both bags at the same time. He was probably trying to show off his strength, but the gesture was lost on Vee.

Okay, so maybe it wasn't quite *lost* because she'd obviously noticed. It was hard *not* to notice the solid muscles across his arms and shoulders. But a good man was made up of more than his muscles, and she knew what kind of man Ben was.

Ben had broken her best friend's heart. Olivia had stayed in bed for a week depressed and crying over their breakup, which was all Ben's fault. Vee wasn't in any hurry to forgive him for that, no matter how good he looked in a T-shirt and jeans.

"Where do you want it?" Ben asked. He nodded his square chin toward the bag of soil under his arm.

"Right here is fine," she answered, sweeping her arm indistinctly toward the ground at her feet.

Grunting with the effort—or possibly just for the effect the sound gave—he dropped the bag of potting soil where she'd indicated and then lowered the fertilizer bag near the closest flower bed.

"I'd appreciate it if you'd do the flower beds first," she said, deciding there was no reason not to be civil with Ben since he'd offered to help—as a non-paid apprentice. "I've got a dozen rosebushes in the back of the truck that I'll be planting in those beds today."

"Yeah, I noticed them when I was getting the soil. Do you want me to bring those back here for you, too?"

"Eventually. For now, just dig."

"Pink and red," he said, sounding like he was just making conversation. "Did you pick out those colors, or was it my mother?"

"Your mother, actually. I've planned most of the landscaping colors palette, but she specifically asked for red and pink roses. Red for love. Pink for gratitude. She said it would remind her every day to be thankful for her family."

"That sounds like my mother," Ben murmured.

"I'll get these planters finished and then we'll worry about the rosebushes. After that you can turn the earth for the garden and I can start seeding behind you," she said, pulling on her gardening gloves and picking up a trowel.

She reached for the first tray of yellow mums and easily fell into her task. She'd organized the flowers and seeds according to the layout print she'd prepared of the Atwoods' backyard. She'd spent a long time planning what would go where according to the palettes she'd created. She loved seeing the way the colors came together to make a final product she could be proud of and the Atwoods would enjoy. It was her artist's canvas, available for everyone to see and appreciate.

Ben let out a low wolf whistle as he surveyed her print. She hadn't realized he was standing over her shoulder. He was supposed to be digging.

"That looks complicated," he commented. "And here I thought we were just playing around in the dirt."

"It's a lot more than that," she fired back before taking a deep breath and reminding herself that she'd decided to be civil. "It's actually quite interesting, or at least it is to me. The vegetable garden itself is determined by what your mom and dad want to grow, of course, but you get a better yield, not to mention a better aesthetic experience, if you know which vegetables should be planted next to each other for optimum growth and health. We're going to do green beans, snap peas, carrots and tomatoes for starters."

She gulped in a breath of air and continued enthusiastically. It didn't take much for her to warm to her subject. "As for the hanging baskets, I not only consider which blossoms develop well in this area, but also the arrangement of color palettes..."

She hadn't realized she'd launched into a full-throttle landscaping lecture until she noticed the pensive look on Ben's face. Clearly his mind had wandered, and she flushed at the realization that she'd probably been boring him to tears.

"And...you really don't care a whit about color palettes. Sorry. Too much information," she said with a wince and a guarded chuckle. "I forget that not everyone is as ardent about gardening as I am."

"Don't apologize. I am interested. It's just that what you said reminded me of a friend of mine who—"

He broke off his sentence as suddenly as he'd started it, his eyes widening to enormous proportions, as if he'd almost said something monumental, something he'd regret. He definitely looked a little green around the gills.

"A friend of yours who…?" she prompted, curious as to why he had stopped speaking so suddenly. She usually wasn't the nosey type, preferring to mind her own business and give others the same courtesy. But he'd started it, and now she wanted him to finish.

"She—er—works in flowers. I can't really tell you much more than that, I mean about her career." He turned his back to her and scanned the flower bed. "Is it all right if I just rip into this bag any way I want, or is there a secret procedure I'm not aware of?"

Clearly he was deflecting. Vee was tempted to press the issue just to stir things up a bit, but she refrained. Once he'd finished breaking Olivia's heart, Ben's female "friends" had become no business of hers.

"No special instructions," she informed him. "Just try to open it so too much of the fertilizer doesn't spill out all at once."

"Got it," he said, flashing her a smile.

Who was this elusive *she* who worked with flowers? Vee wondered in spite of herself. He sounded as if he truly cared for her, whoever she was. Maybe he'd learned his lesson and matured some. Or maybe he'd met a woman who hadn't immediately fallen prey to his charms, and it had forced him to actually put some effort into a relationship. But if that was the case, this woman must really be something special. She would have to be a classic beauty. Vee could almost picture the woman—long, flowing blond hair and perfect makeup that accentuated deep cheekbones and a perfect chin.

The exact opposite of Vee, in other words. No one could call her heart-shaped face *classic*. The dimple in her chin marred any chance for that. At best, she could be called pretty— but it wasn't the sort of pretty anyone noticed. She was way too easily overlooked for reasons that had nothing to do with her diminutive height. Her strength was her intelligence, not her beauty, and men didn't line up at the door to date smart women. At least in her experience—or lack of—they didn't.

Which mattered *why?*

She scoffed inwardly and turned her mind back to her work. She wasn't going to consider any other possibility except that she might be nursing her own curiosity. And even that felt inappropriate. She shouldn't care one bit about Ben or about any women that he knew and might care for.

At the end of the day, Ben was still the man who'd broken the heart of her best friend. That hadn't and wouldn't change. Unfortunately for

Ben, Vee had a long memory, and though she knew God would want her to forgive him, she just wasn't there yet.

It might have been easier if Ben had hurt *Vee* and not her friend. She could shake off an injury to herself, but going after someone she loved—that was stepping over the mark. She tended to go all mama tiger on anyone who hurt her friends and loved ones.

And by "anyone" she meant Ben.

Vee shook her head and jammed the trowel into the bag of soil, perhaps a bit more forcefully than was absolutely necessary. With a renewed effort, she set to work, trying to keep her mind focused on the task at hand and not the man turning the earth just a few feet to her left.

To her surprise, she and Ben worked well together. After Ben had turned the soil, they retrieved the rosebushes from the truck. It was nice to have an extra pair of hands. Planting went smoothly and much quicker than Vee had anticipated.

Then they moved their combined attention to the plot for the vegetable garden. Ben flipped over the dense spring turf and mixed it with fertilizer while Vee followed along behind him, planting seeds with her trowel.

They didn't speak much, but that was just as well. Vee didn't know what to say to him, and she hated it when she felt like she needed to chatter just to fill up the space. She wasn't much for small talk.

Before she knew it, the entire afternoon had passed and the sun was starting to make its descent in the west. Vee glanced at her watch and was surprised to find it was after six o'clock in the evening. Where had the time gone?

"I think it's about quitting time," she said, tapping the face of her watch. "I'll be back to finish what's left tomorrow. I appreciate all your help today. I wouldn't have gotten nearly this far without you."

Ben wiped the sweat off his forehead with the edge of his shirt, then rubbed his palms together and grimaced.

"What's wrong with your hand?" she asked, reaching out to examine his left palm.

"It's nothing. I just got a couple of blisters." Stubbornly, he drew his hand into a fist to prevent her from examining it.

"Let me see." He refused at first, keeping his hand tightly clenched, but she ignored his protests and gently worked his fingers open so she could scrutinize his wound.

"See? It's not so bad," he muttered through gritted teeth. "No big deal."

"Maybe not," she answered in a conciliatory tone, "but you need to clean your palm so it doesn't get infected. You stay there," she said, pointing to a porch chair. "I'll be back in a jiffy."

She entered the house through the sliding door in the back and brushed her shoes against the welcome mat. "Excuse me, Mrs. Atwood?"

"You're still here?" asked Ben's mom in surprise as she entered the room. "I would have thought you'd have something better to do on a Friday night than hang around here, especially if you're not on call at the fire station. Don't tell me there's no fancy date with a handsome hunk?"

Vee blushed so hard she thought her head might pop. "No, ma'am. Not tonight."

Not *ever,* actually, but Vee didn't see the need to elaborate on the subject.

Ben's mother chuckled lightly. "Their loss."

"Yes, ma'am," she agreed, becoming more embarrassed by the moment. She decided to change the subject before it got completely out of control. "I was wondering if you had any rubbing alcohol or hydrogen peroxide that I could use. Ben has a few blisters on his hands, and I'd hate for them to get infected."

"Of course. My son isn't used to shoveling dirt, poor dear. Why don't you sit down for a moment while I get them for you?" His mom sounded more amused than concerned by her son's dire plight. She gestured to a chair at the dining room table, but Vee politely declined. Despite the woman's kindness, Vee decided it was better for her to remain standing on the mat where she wouldn't accidentally make a mess with her dirty clothing.

In less than a minute, Ben's mother returned with a bottle of rubbing alcohol, a roll of gauze, a handful of large cotton balls and a tube of antibacterial cream, delivered with a perceptive smile.

"There you go, hon. Everything you need to patch my boy up right."

"This ought to do it," Vee agreed warmly. Ben's mother was one of the most pleasant women she knew. "Thank you so much, Mrs. Atwood."

"Never a problem. You tell Ben that his mother said that he ought to wear gloves next time."

Vee chuckled. "Oh, don't worry. I will." How nice, to have his mother's permission to rub it in a little bit, both literally and figuratively.

Laden with her impromptu medical kit, she returned to where Ben waited, tucked onto a porch chair with his legs extended before him, crossed at the ankles. His head was back, his eyes were closed and his chest was rising and falling evenly. Vee thought he might be asleep and wondered if she ought to wake him, but when she approached, his eyes, with those thick, long eyelashes that only men ever seemed blessed with, fluttered open.

His gaze narrowed on her tentatively when he saw the bottle of rubbing alcohol in her hand.

"Rubbing alcohol? That wouldn't have been my first choice." He sounded none too thrilled about it.

"Don't be a baby. Now put out your hand."

Ben frowned but allowed her to pry the fingers of his left hand open, palm upward.

Vee doused a cotton ball in rubbing alcohol, cupped his hand in hers and began dabbing at the red, angry blisters that covered his palm.

"Ow," Ben complained, trying to pull his hand out of her grip. "That hurts."

Vee persisted in wiping the wounds, ignoring his protests. "If you insist on pulling away like that, it's going to take a lot longer to get this done."

"You're enjoying this, aren't you?" he asked suspiciously. "You're making it hurt on purpose."

Was he teasing her? Maybe. She couldn't tell, so she went for a neutral—though truthful—response. "Of course not. I would never do that."

Vee carefully wrapped his hand in strips of gauze so he couldn't accuse her of further assaults on his person. "There. All better. Just keep it clean, okay? Doctor's orders."

"Hey, are you forgetting who the paramedic is here?"

"Fine, then—mother's orders. If you don't like it, take it up with your mom. She's the one who gave me the supplies to get you bandaged up. And if you don't keep that gauze clean, you'll be answering to her."

"Do you really think I can do that? I work with cars, remember?"

"That could be an issue. I don't know how you're going to avoid grease when you're tinkering with a car engine. I suppose you'll just have to do the best you can."

"I will," he promised, but under his breath he muttered, "I'm glad you're a firefighter and not a nurse."

"That makes two of us. I didn't try to hurt you on purpose, but I'll be the first to admit my bedside manner is a little rough."

"A little?" He chuckled and shook his head. "If that's what you're like when you're trying to help me then I'd hate to think of the damage you could do if you really were trying to hurt me."

Hurt you like you hurt Olivia? Vee thought to herself. He must have noticed the shift in her expression that accompanied the new direction of her thoughts because he quickly changed the subject.

"Now that the work's done—the planting and the bandaging—would you like to stay for dinner? I know I told you I can't cook, and I can't, but even I can manage to throw a couple of steaks on the grill without ruining them. Mama usually ropes me into grilling for her when the weather cooperates, so I'm guessing that's probably what she has in mind for today. We've got plenty of room at the table for one more, and I'm sure my parents would love for you to stay and visit the family."

"I should be offering *you* a steak dinner for all the help you've been to me today. I wouldn't have gotten even a quarter as far along as we did together."

"No problem. I was glad to help. It was for a good cause. And we do work well together."

He sounded as surprised as she felt. Vee shivered in what she thought must be discomfort, though in truth she didn't dare identify the emotion. Is that what Ben thought, that they *worked well together?*

"As for dinner," she said and then paused. She already had other plans. Not an in-person date with a handsome hunk who wanted to take her to dinner or out to the movies like Ben's mother had suggested, but definitely the next best thing. Those *plans* in question were calling to her, tugging at her heartstrings to make short work of leaving and hurry along to Cup o' Jo Café.

But then there was Ben, with his convincing half smile and dancing gaze. She hesitated.

Vee couldn't believe she was tempted, even for a moment, to stick around and share a dinner with Ben and his family—but she was. No wonder Olivia had fallen for the man hook, line and sinker. Ben could be very charismatic when he wanted to be.

Nice, even. And he was good-looking, no denying that fact.

Which was *exactly* why she had to say no.

She took a deep breath and plunged in before she lost what was left of her mental faculties and caved to his suggestion.

"I'm sorry, Ben," she murmured, pausing only for a moment at his crestfallen look. If she didn't know any better, she would think he actually cared what her answer would be.

But that wouldn't change it. "As much as I'd love to share a meal with you and your parents this evening," she continued, "I already have other plans."

Chapter Four

Dear BJ,

This week has been very tough for me. Sometimes I just feel like I need to let my hair down—do you know what I mean? I'm so guarded all the time, worrying about what people think of me and, even more, what they expect of me. I'm afraid I might not be living up to everyone's standards.

It's stressful keeping everything bottled up inside all the time. It would be nice to be able to see things differently for a change, from another point of view. From a different set of eyes.

Oh, who am I kidding? I am what I am and that's all…well, you know. I'm starting to sound like Popeye now. Terrific. Who ever knew that he was such a sage?

I guess I should just accept the way that

God made me and not try to make myself anything different. I might feel like a distinct person inside my heart, but people don't see that, do they?

That's never going to change. I'm never going to change.

It's just that when I read your emails, I feel… well, differently about myself. Stronger. I wish I could be as easygoing as you obviously are.

I downloaded the graphics you sent me. They're really good! I'm attaching a revised script that incorporates the photographs, so we can begin preparing the final presentation. Let me know if you have any modifications you'd like me to make.

Faithfully,

Veronica Jayne

The rich smells of roasted coffee, nutmeg and baked apples warmed Vee's nostrils as she entered the Cup o' Jo Café. She inhaled deeply and the tension she always carried around in her shoulders and neck was immediately soothed by the colorful, welcoming atmosphere. The familiar quiet buzz of the other patrons talking as they sat in booths enjoying a hot meal heartened her. Cup o' Jo had been a regular hangout for Vee growing up, and even now it was her go-to place when she needed a lift in spirits.

Or a computer with internet service. Tonight, she needed both. She couldn't wait to see if BJ had replied to her last post.

Jo Murphy Spencer, the owner of the café, approached in her usual exuberant way, her red curls bouncing and her smile beaming. The woman never failed to put Vee at ease, no matter how she was feeling when she walked in the door. Jo, with her wacky T-shirts, observant nature and ear for the latest gossip, was like a second mother to most of the town. Vee suspected the older woman knew more about her than most of her friends and neighbors did, but she was okay with that. There was no one better than Jo for doling out sound advice, solicited or not.

"Vee, dear," Jo exclaimed, waving the purple dishcloth she held in one hand. "Have you come to spend some time on the internet for your Spanish class, or shall I seat you at a table for a nice home-style dinner?"

Vee felt her face warm and hoped Jo didn't notice the flush of her cheeks. Not much chance of that, though. Jo was extremely perceptive. She was bound to see that something was off, but to Vee's relief, Jo did nothing more than raise a curious brow.

She was here for the computer, all right, but despite the fact that she had an assignment due the following day that she needed to type up and submit, her Spanish course was the last thing on her mind.

"I'll just slip in behind the computer in the corner if that one's available," Vee said, indicating what looked like an open spot in the straight line of tables across the back wall.

"Coffee? Or do you want something more substantial to feed your brain while you work?"

"A caramel latte would be nice."

"Skinny?"

"No, I think I need the real thing tonight," Vee said on a sigh.

"Coming right up," Jo said, tossing her rag onto her left shoulder and bustling over to the service window behind the counter. "I need a big slice of apple pie, Phoebe, dear," she called.

"But I didn't—" Vee started to protest.

Jo waved her away. "On the house, dear. You look like you could use a little something to perk you up, and there ain't nothing like a slice of one of Phoebe's famous pies to do just that."

Vee chuckled and nodded. It was useless to try to argue with Jo when the woman had her mind set on something. All that would do was delay the inevitable. Besides, Vee had planned on ordering dinner here eventually, and apple pie was her favorite.

Tonight, she would start with dessert. After

the day she'd just had, she thought she deserved it.

She weaved her way through the tables to the back corner, greeting everyone she passed. Serendipity was a small town. Everybody literally knew everybody—and usually knew everybody's business—which was part of the reason Vee was so hush-hush regarding her own plans for the future and most especially her potential internet sweetheart. Even her closest friends might accidentally blurt out the truth if they knew about it—which was exactly why they didn't.

Sliding in behind the computer, she wiggled the mouse to bring the screen out of sleep mode and signed on, first to the college website where her Spanish class was held, and then onto her private email account. Were anyone to come around to speak to her, she could easily toggle the screen so her class work covered her email and save herself from any possible embarrassment or awkwardness.

It was a clandestine moment. She felt almost as if she were taking part in a spy novel. Secret messages. Covert engagements.

Even if they *were* only online.

It was still fun. And perfectly harmless, right?

Vee's heart raced when she saw that there

was a message from BJ. She had nearly a hundred other emails—mostly junk mail mixed
with some from friends and classmates—but
they went unnoticed as she clicked the one and
only link of true importance to her.

Dear Veronica Jayne,
I'll take a look at the revisions you sent for class
later tonight, but right now I'm more intrigued
by what you said about yourself. I've been
thinking about you a lot recently. I think you
should do it. No, really, you ought to do it! Put
your hair down, I mean, figuratively speaking.
Or maybe literally, too, for all I know.

Do you wear your hair down all the time?
That's how I picture you. Long, cascading
hair. Pretty eyes. Flowery dresses that course
around your ankles in waves.

Am I close? Or am I putting you on the
spot?

Even without being able to see you, I can
tell what a wonderful person you are. God
made you special, Veronica. You need to believe in yourself more—and allow others to
believe in you, as well.
I know I do.
Take care,
BJ

Vee leaned back in her seat and smoothed her hair back into a knot at her neck as she let out a deep breath that she hoped was not as audible as it felt.

BJ thought she was *special*.

They may not have ever met in person, but he *cared* for her. If Vee's face had been pink-stained before, it was no doubt a flaming red now.

Her heart and her mind were all over the place, fluttering and diving and soaring. Was it a slip of the fingers? Was any of this real? Could she have feelings for a man she'd technically never met?

She'd heard stories of internet romance, of course, but could it seriously happen to her? Could she truly meet Mr. Right online? She highly doubted it, and yet there was a small part of her that hoped for it to be so.

BJ was good to her, not to mention *for* her. Without even trying, he encouraged her to admit to her true feelings about herself and the world, emotions she usually stuffed way, *way* down inside her heart and mind.

How did he do that?

It was unsettling but in a good way. No one else knew her private thoughts and feelings the way he did.

But *cascading hair? Floral dresses?* What could be further from the truth? Would he be disappointed if they met in person and he learned that she was so far from what he had imagined?

No one except her own family had ever seen her wearing her hair down, in a literal sense. She'd been wearing her hair in a knot since the beginning of junior high school when the popular girls had picked on her for being a tomboy. In Vee's contrary way, her defense had been to be exactly that, and so from then on, her thick, dark hair was always pulled tightly into a bun at the nape of her neck.

But that was a long time ago. She wasn't facing junior high drama anymore, so what did the way she wore her hair even matter anymore?

Maybe BJ was right. Maybe she should—

"Hey, Vee." Ben's rich baritone voice startled her and she bolted upright in her seat as if she'd touched a live electrical wire. "I'm surprised to see you here. Didn't you say you had plans for dinner tonight? I thought maybe you had a date or something."

"Ben," she exclaimed, laying a hand on her racing heart as he slid into the chair across from her. Her pulse roared in her head as, in a panic, she clumsily moused over the *X* that closed the browser completely.

Well, that was smooth. She'd been so lost in her thoughts that she hadn't seen him standing next to her. How long had he been there? Had he seen the email?

She'd probably drawn attention to herself with all of her jumping and jerking, but if he suspected anything was amiss, he didn't say so.

As a matter of fact, he didn't say anything at all. He just leaned his elbows on the table, staring at her over the top of the computer monitor, his bronze-green eyes unreadable. Vee wasn't sure how long it was until Jo arrived at the table with a serving tray in her hands, but her interruption was an unquestionable relief. Vee hadn't realized she was holding her breath until Jo spoke and dissolved the tension in the air.

"Coffee and fresh apple pie for each of you," Jo said, disrupting the silence as she served them.

"Thank you, Jo," Ben said, squaring the plate of pie in front of him and picking up his fork. "This looks delicious. But, uh, what about dinner?" he asked, directing his question toward Vee. "Is pie going to do it for you? No wonder you're so tiny."

Vee straightened her spine and tipped her chin. So what if she was small in stature? It wasn't from eating dessert instead of her regular meals. She glared at him.

Jo, as always, could read Vee well enough to pick up on the tension and interrupted once again. "Meatloaf, mashed potatoes and green beans are the house special tonight," she tempted. "My nephew makes a mean batch of home-style potatoes and gravy."

Ben and Vee nodded simultaneously, and Vee realized just how hungry she really was when her stomach growled at the offering. She'd been so distracted by BJ's email that she hadn't been paying attention to her rumbling tummy.

If *she* was hungry, she realized belatedly, then Ben must be famished. He'd pulled more than his share of the weight helping her break in the soil for the garden. It was still tough this time of year.

"What happened to your steak dinner?" she asked as soon as Jo left the table to put in their orders. "I thought you and your parents had something going."

He shrugged and shook his head, causing a dark curl to fall forward onto his brow. The right side of his mouth twitched upward. "As it turned out, my parents already had dinner plans with another couple," he explained. "Apparently they're following some reality television show or other together. Can you imagine? I would never have pegged my parents for something like that." He chuckled. "Anyway, I didn't want to eat alone, so here I am. And you?"

"I have a date."

He raised a brow.

She couldn't help but chuckle. "With my computer. I've got some…stuff I need to catch up on." That was vague enough, right?

"Landscaping?"

She shrugged noncommittally. She was a dinosaur who still did most of her landscaping the old-fashioned way—sketching by hand—but Ben didn't need to know that.

"I've got to say I'm impressed by that *stuff.* I had no idea that planting a garden could be so complicated. Or so interesting."

"Not to mention fun," she added, warming to the conversation. "Come on, you can admit it. You enjoyed digging in the dirt with me. Isn't that every little boy's fantasy come to life?"

His eyes widened and his gaze danced, and she realized that her words *might* have come out sounding flirtatious—which of course wasn't her intention.

She was suddenly aware—*very* aware—of the tension, like an electrical charge in the atmosphere between them. Something had shifted. Changed. *Warmed.* And she couldn't break her gaze away from Ben's to save her life.

It was Ben who finally looked away, taking

a slow, deliberate sip of his coffee. His smile, however, did not disappear. If anything, it grew stronger.

"So, then," he asked casually, "did you want me to find another table for dinner? I'd hate to bother you if you're—busy."

She wanted to say he should leave. She knew she *should* bow out gracefully. He'd generously given her that out on a platter. And yet… And yet. He'd been generous with his time today, and his efforts on helping her with the gardening. He'd been patient and hardworking. Companionable, even.

"No, of course not. Please stay."

This was way, *way* better than steak. Not the meatloaf, though that was good, too, but mostly it was the company Ben was keeping. And he couldn't have been more surprised than if he were enjoying a meal with Attila the Hun.

Vee Bishop usually took a swipe at him at every turn, but tonight he was discovering that she could be warm and sweet when she wanted to be. He'd always known she was an intelligent woman with a great deal of inner strength, but spending time with her, both gardening and at dinner, had enlightened him in more ways than one.

He'd always considered her a little bit edgy—

which she definitely was—but it hadn't even occurred to him to wonder about what else went on in that tough-girl brain of hers, that there might be other sides to her that he was missing.

Not until today, anyway.

"My sister Kayla's coming into town for a few days," he commented before forking a bite of mashed potatoes into his mouth and groaning in pleasure at the delightfully creamy home-made texture. "She's bringing my two nephews with her."

Vee made a surprised sound from the bottom of her throat. "To be honest, I didn't even remember that you had a sister until you said something just now."

"No, you probably wouldn't. She's several years older than me, so you wouldn't have been in any classes with her. She moved away just out of high school—out of state, actually, to California—to get a political science degree from Stanford. After that, she was off at law school and once she passed her bar exam, she was immediately swept up by a hotshot San Francisco law firm. I'm incredibly proud of her, of course, but I do wish I could see her and the kids more often. She rarely gets home, and I don't get much of a chance to go visit her in California. Of course, my mom and dad are thrilled to be able to see their grandsons again."

"I'm sure. Are you planning anything special for your nephews while they're here?"

"I'm looking forward to tossing a football around with the boys. Kayla's a single mother, so they're always raring to play sports when they visit home. And the church carnival is coming up. I expect they'll enjoy popping balloons with a dart and maybe winning a goldfish in a plastic bag for their effort, if memory serves me right."

"Which I'm sure your sister will appreciate," she added wryly.

Ben chuckled. "You're probably right about that one. I can't imagine that toting goldfish back to California is in Kayla's short-term plans—or her long-term plans, for that matter. I'll most likely have to keep them at my apartment, where the boys can visit them when they're in town."

"That would be nice of you." She gave him a speculative look, as if she was trying to figure him out. It made him uncomfortable, and he cleared his throat.

"I don't mind. I can be a responsible pet owner—now. Not like when I named Tinker or anything. I wouldn't forget to feed the fish if I put them in a glass bowl on my counter." His mind drifted to a happy memory from his own childhood. "I remember as a kid how excited I was to attend the church carnival every year. It was such a big moment in my life, throwing a ring around a pop bottle and winning a prize."

"I remember being at the carnival, too," admitted Vee. "Although I don't think I ever ringed any pop bottles. I'm not sure I ever won any prizes to speak of."

"I'll have to win one for you this year at the carnival, then. Maybe a big stuffed teddy bear or something." With his impulsive streak—the one that had gotten him into trouble more times than he could count—he'd spoken before he'd even taken a moment to consider what he was actually saying.

Now, judging from the stunned look on Vee's face, he had to find some way to backpedal.

"You probably don't want a stuffed animal," he continued, but that only seemed to make things worse. Vee turned an alarming shade of red. "I imagine you aren't the type of woman to have a room full of bears and unicorns."

She had taken a long pull of her water right as he began speaking, and now she choked on it.

"And…I should shut up now," he finished.

She sputtered and shook her head. "Your nephews," she gasped when she was able.

"Right. I was telling you about Felix and Nigel. They both want to hang around with me at work. They're at an age where they're in complete awe of what I do."

"Being a paramedic? I'll bet. With all the bells and whistles—literally—it's pretty exciting stuff."

Ben cracked a grin. "I meant my job as an auto mechanic, actually. They want me to let them get under the hood of a car and get low-down and greasy. You know how little boys are."

Her gaze softened. "I remember. My brothers were like that, too. They were always coming to the supper table covered head to toe with dirt, and Mama wouldn't let them sit down to eat until they were clean right down to under their fingernails."

Suddenly self-conscious, Ben clasped his hands into his lap underneath the table. The dirge of being a grease monkey was the complete inability to get his hands clean, especially under the nails, no matter what products and brushes he used. Although that might be fun for a nine-and seven-year-old boy, it was not so much for a thirty-year-old man having dinner with a pretty woman.

Even if she was a woman who didn't like him.

"You have the oddest expression on your face," she remarked, her dark brows closing in over her nose as she eyed him questioningly. "What are you thinking about?"

"Grease," he blurted, cringing as he returned his hands to the tabletop. As embarrassing as it might be to have dirty nails, he'd hardly be able to finish his meal without using his hands. He suddenly pictured himself diving headlong into his mashed potatoes like a man in a pie-eating contest, a thought that gave him an inward laugh. Somehow he expected that might be even more conspicuous than a little stubborn grease on his hands.

To his relief, Vee merely chuckled at his blurted exclamation.

"That would be one of the hazards of your job, I suppose. I've got a similar problem myself sometimes, so I'm not one to complain. You'd be amazed how filthy I can get when I garden all day, jamming my hands into potting soil and dirt, even with protective gloves on. You shower and scrub, and still all the grime doesn't quite come off."

Her answer, and the affable laughter that followed, put Ben immediately at ease—at least until another unpleasant thought popped into his head.

What would Veronica Jayne think about having dinner with a man who couldn't even get his hands clean?

When Ben pictured some well-into-the-future dinner date with Veronica Jayne, it was in some classy, expensive restaurant where a coat and tie were mandatory and the prices weren't even listed on the menu.

It would be nothing as simple as enjoying a good old-fashioned home-style meal at Cup o' Jo, like he was now with Vee, that was for sure. The very thought of taking Veronica Jayne to an upscale restaurant such as he suspected she was accustomed to made the hair on the back of his neck stand on edge.

He'd have to wear a suit. With a *tie*.

His throat constricted involuntarily, nearly cutting off his air, and he heaved in a deep, ragged breath to compensate. Christmas and Easter church services were the *only* times he subjected himself to the misery of a sports jacket and necktie. Ugh and double ugh with a cherry on top.

Keep breathing, he coached himself. He was getting way ahead of himself here. It wasn't like he and Veronica Jayne were going to be going on a date *anywhere* anytime soon, if at all. At this point their relationship hardly qualified as a romance. It was a warm friendship… with potential. The prospect of romance was there, even if the reality wasn't.

"I'm glad you don't mind the grease," he said,

forcing his mind back to the woman seated across from him. Vee deserved his full attention, especially now that they were official dinner partners. How he had gone from trying to hide the grease under his nails from Vee Bishop to practically walking down the aisle with Veronica Jayne was beyond him. He mentally shook himself to put himself back in the game.

"Not a problem." When Vee smiled at him—truly, fully smiled at him for the first time he could remember—Ben felt it all the way to his toes, and for a moment all of his thoughts about Veronica Jayne and dinners in expensive restaurants faded completely.

Which came as a surprise even to him. What could that possibly be about?

He was grateful, he supposed, that she hadn't up and left him at the dinner table with his wandering mind and greasy fingernails.

Yeah. That was it.

Grateful.

It couldn't possibly be more. Could it?

Chapter Five

Dear BJ,

Thanks for the note and the encouragement. Take whatever time you need to modify the content I sent you for our project. You're the presentation-software whiz, after all. At the end of the day, you've got the harder part of the undertaking—putting it all together cohesively. Once again I'm thankful I got paired with you.

I've been praying about what you said, and I have decided that I'm actually going to do it! I'm really going to put myself out there for a change and see what happens, though let me tell you, it was no easy decision for me to decide to expose my true self for others to see. I can't even put into words how nervous I am, but I know you're right. I can't keep living this way. I can't serve God to the best of my ability if I'm too busy worrying about what other people think about me. I've got to get over it once and for all. The truth is, I've had walls up nearly all my life.

You're the one who has finally helped me break them down. Thank you for that.

Truly yours,

Veronica Jayne

When Vee decided to do something, she never did it halfway. Go big or go home, as the saying went. If she was going to change her appearance and let people see the *real Vee,* she was going to do it right.

Hair. Eyebrows. Nails. The works. Frankly, it sounded horribly uncomfortable at best, and blatantly painful at worst. But she was committed now, and that was that.

It was Tuesday, and she had the day off both from Emerson's Hardware and the fire station, so she decided to head for Amarillo, hoping to be able to pick up the most important facet on which her entire plan hinged—and the one thing she absolutely did not have.

A dress.

When Vee was little, her mother had put her in frilly dresses for special occasions, but once she got old enough to pick clothes for herself, dresses and skirts simply weren't going to happen. Not in her wardrobe. She'd always worn slacks, even to church services, including weddings, funerals, Christmas and Easter. She wasn't a girly-girl, and she'd never seen the point of owning a dress if she was never going to wear one. Dresses weren't her style.

At least not yet. Maybe it was like her habit of pulling back her hair—a relic of a choice she'd made years ago, a choice she might be ready to outgrow. She'd never know unless she tried. And tried *quickly* because she only had a week to pull the whole thing—or rather, pull *herself*—together.

Every year on the Saturday before Easter the police and fire departments, in conjunction with the ladies' charity group from church, hosted a special dinner for the less fortunate in Serendipity and the surrounding areas. It was one of the highlights of the year for Serendipity. The town folk were always generous in their donations, and the meal was generally an enormous success. This would be Vee's first year in the middle of the action.

Less than one week wasn't a good deal of time to make any kind of personal transformation, much less the kind of makeover Vee had in mind, and she was all on her own in this. No fairy godmother to wave her wand like in the story of Cinderella. Not her friends. She

knew better than to let them in on it. If anyone
so much as cracked a joke about what she was
doing—and they would—she knew herself well
enough to know she'd bail on her plan.

So that left no one, not even her mother to
help her. And oh, how that fact burned through
her chest. How much easier this would be if
Mama was still around to put the finishing
touches on Vee herself.

Still, she reminded herself, she wasn't completely alone. She had the Lord, and in the long
run, He was really the reason she was doing this
at all. Hopefully through Christ she would discover the courage to find herself amid all the
fluctuation in her life right now and be able to
anchor herself in God for the long haul, including stateside mission work.

Lately, she'd been clinging to the verses in
Matthew 5, especially verse 16. *Let your light
so shine before men, that they may see your
good works and glorify your Father in heaven.*

Wasn't that exactly what she was trying to
do? Let her light shine? Step out from behind
the shields she'd used to protect herself from
ridicule or rejection and let the world see who
she truly was?

Those verses filled her with renewed hope
and peace—and most of all, courage. She
knew she couldn't do this herself—but then,

she didn't have to, did she? She had God in her corner, and what more could a woman ask for?

She started humming an old Sunday school ditty that had abruptly come to mind. Before she knew it, she was singing the silly children's song out loud, tapping her fingers on the steering wheel in time to the music.

"This little light of mine, I'm going to let it shine, let it shine, let it shine, let it shine."

Or she was going to try, in any case. She might end up glowing no brighter than the muted headlights on her old, reliable truck, but by golly, she was going to give it her best shot or die of embarrassment trying.

Her happy, sunshine-filled day lasted until she got about ten minutes out of town, when the engine on her customarily peppy little black truck suddenly sputtered and wheezed like an old man with a cold.

"Oh, no," Vee groaned aloud, glancing down to check the dashboard panel. She'd filled the gas tank just before she'd left town, and she had recently checked the fluid levels for the oil and antifreeze.

What could be wrong?

Please, God, let it be nothing.

But it wasn't nothing. It was *everything,* apparently. Which just figured. Every light on the panel suddenly blinked red, and then she no longer felt the power of the transmission beneath her feet. Holding the steering wheel tightly, she carefully guided the truck to the side of the road with what insignificant momentum was left in it.

Great. Just what she needed—to have her truck break down in the middle of nowhere, on a highway that was rarely used even by commercial vehicles. Add to that the fact that this was really her only day to spend an entire afternoon in Amarillo searching for the perfect dress.

Not her best day.

With a loud, exasperated sigh, she slid out from behind the wheel and marched forward to open the hood, leaning forward and peering inside to see if she could discern any problems offhand.

Which, of course, she couldn't, and she didn't have any notion of why she'd looked at all.

Like she knew the first thing about engines. Who was she kidding? All she knew how to do was change the oil and check the fluid levels, and she wasn't particularly skillful at those two things. She absently rubbed at her forehead, where a throbbing headache was rapidly developing.

At least she wasn't being stubborn about it. Calm, cool and sensible. That was Vee. It took her less than thirty seconds to acknowledge the truth. She was officially stranded and it was time to call in for reinforcements.

She mumbled under her breath as she fished her cell phone out of her back pocket and checked for reception, only to find that there were no bars.

Not one, single, solitary bar. She growled in frustration. Of course there was no reception on such a tiny stretch of uninhabited road. Why would there be?

Why was this happening to her, especially now? Couldn't she catch a break just this once? But then, why should this time be any different than the others for her? Nothing was ever easy for her. It never had been. Scaling brick walls had become her specialty, both literally and figuratively.

She sighed again, even louder this time. At this rate she would have to flag down a trucker—assuming, of course, that one would drive by. More than likely she'd be sitting on the road for quite some time.

Not exactly how she'd planned to spend her day.

Holding her cell phone as high as she could reach in the air, which wasn't saying much at her five feet two inches, she walked around in ever-increasing circles, watching for bars to appear in the corner of her phone, turning this way and that in an unscripted cellular-tower dance that left her feeling silly and embarrassed.

If someone saw her now, how they would laugh, watching her waving her phone in the air as if that would somehow make any difference in the signal strength. It was a hopeless cause, as well she knew.

She'd just decided to return to her truck and wait for a Good Samaritan to pass by when a single bar flickered in the upper-left corner of her phone.

"Yes!" she exclaimed, freezing in place so she would not lose the signal. "Hold it..." she squeaked, "please, God, let the signal hold until I can dial someone to come pick me up."

She paused, her arm still extended high in the air. Now that she finally had a connection, she wasn't sure who to dial. She didn't have a phone book handy to call the auto shop back in town, and her brother Eli was working his shift at the police station. He'd probably come get her if she asked, but she didn't want him to neglect his duties, and it wasn't like it was an emergency for 911.

At least, not yet, it wasn't. The future remained to be seen.

At length, she settled on calling her father.

She knew he hadn't left the house much since her mother had died, but she was certain he'd make an exception for her.

However, after speaking to him and tossing around a few other options, they decided that it would be better for him to call Derek's Auto Garage where Ben worked and have them meet her here with a tow truck. They'd be able to bring her truck back into town with them and not leave it temporarily abandoned on the side of the highway.

The sooner they started fixing it, the sooner they would be finished. Vee groaned at the thought of an expensive car repair bill. Yet another stress point she didn't need right now, but since she used her truck for work, it was a necessity to get it fixed as soon as possible.

The sun was shining and it was a nice, temperate spring day in Texas, so Vee yanked down the tailgate of her truck and perched herself, legs swinging off the edge, to wait for the tow. She wished she had a book to read. Who knew how long it would be before the tow truck showed up? Her best guess was that she was a good twenty miles from town, and tow truck drivers were notorious for taking their own sweet time. She figured she might as well enjoy the fresh air while she waited.

In truth, it was little time at all. She was surprised when a scant fifteen minutes later she heard the rumbling of a tow truck thundering down the highway.

She was even more surprised to find that it was Ben Atwood behind the wheel, accompanied by two black-haired, green-eyed boys. Of course, she'd known that he worked at his uncle Derek's garage, but she had no idea that he was the tow truck operator, too.

She smiled at the wiggling youngsters as Ben pulled his truck next to hers. Even a casual observer could see the kids were clearly related to Ben. They must be his nephews, Vee thought.

Ben pulled in front of her and then backed the tow truck close enough to hook Vee's truck up to it.

"Hey, Vee," he greeted as he stepped out of the cab. "Having a little engine trouble, are we?"

"Apparently," she answered mildly, tongue in cheek. "Thanks for coming so quickly, although I've got to say that I'm surprised to see you here. I didn't know you drove the tow truck," Vee commented as she watched him fasten the chains from one vehicle to the other.

"I don't," he replied, flashing his generous smile. "Not usually, anyway. My uncle has a kid who generally handles tow jobs. But as it happened, I was the one who picked up the phone when your father called, and once I found out it was you…" His sentence drifted to an awkward halt.

Once he'd found out it was her…

What?

He'd made a special trip just to come to her rescue?

"You—uh—have a smudge of grease on your…" He cleared his throat. "Here. Just let me get it." Before she could react, he'd reached forward, gently brushing at her forehead with the pad of his thumb. She held her breath.

"There, then. That's better." Ben swiftly returned his attention to attaching her truck to the towline. His face was flushed a deep copper color, and Vee wondered if the shade was a mark of exertion or uneasiness. His curly brown hair brushed haphazardly across his forehead, as if he'd been running in the wind, giving him an appealing boyish charm. She couldn't help but notice that those enormous biceps of his were straining against his black T-shirt as he worked, only this time he wasn't showing off for her.

At least, she didn't think he was.

Either way, she had to appreciate him as a man. There was no doubt he was strong and attractive, whether he was wearing his paramedic uniform or, as he was now, in blue jeans and a T-shirt. With those amazing green-bronze eyes of his, he was beyond a doubt the best-looking man she'd ever known. She suspected he'd stand out anywhere, but especially in a small town like Serendipity. Certainly he had no shortage of women to date in town.

Which was exactly why she didn't like him. He went through women like bunny rabbits went through carrots, using his razor-sharp teeth to chomp them up and then spit them out. For the first time, she wondered if maybe it wasn't entirely his fault. She was willing to give him at least the hint of the benefit of the doubt, since the women in question practically fell all over themselves to be with him. Of course, that was no excuse for treating them badly, but it had to be a little overwhelming to have so many people want to be with you.

Not that she would know what that felt like.

She apparently scared men silly. Either they didn't like her looks or her attitude. Or both. And she wasn't about to apologize for either, even if she *was* considering making a few changes. In any case, she certainly hadn't been overwhelmed with potential suitors.

Not now. Not ever. So why was Ben paying special attention to her?

That was the question of the hour.

He abruptly raised his head and cocked a

brow. He'd obviously realized that she'd been staring at him, a fact that she hadn't been aware of until the moment their eyes met. He didn't comment on it, though that adorable half-grin of his snuck up one side of his lips, accentuating the dimple in his right cheek and the cleft in his chin. He managed to look both boyishly charming and utterly masculine at the same time.

"I do appreciate this." She had trouble finding the right words to express her gratitude. Maybe because so many other emotions were skirmishing for prominence inside her mind and heart.

"My pleasure," he responded, opening the passenger-side door of the tow truck. "Okay, tough guys. Scoot to the back and buckle up," he ordered his nephews, whom he introduced as nine-year-old Felix and seven-year-old Nigel. It took a moment for him to rein in the squirrelly boys and make sure they were safely buckled into their seats, but then he turned his attention back to Vee. "I hope you don't mind that I brought the kids along for the ride. They wanted to see what their uncle Ben does all day."

Vee didn't mind. Not at all.

The ride back into town was definitely interesting—and informative. For one thing, the boys' presence kept her from the awkwardness of having to be alone with Ben. As a side note, it was interesting to watch him interact with his nephews. The boys hung on his every word as he explained in an age-appropriate fashion how the towing process was executed. He genuinely listened to their questions and answered them carefully. Maybe most telling of all, he laughed out loud at their childish attempts at humor, especially when they were aimed directly at him. He was definitely a man who could take—and make—a joke.

It came as a great surprise to her that Ben was such a natural with children, although she didn't know why he wouldn't be, now that she saw him with his nephews. Both boys clearly desired to emulate him, even going so far as to mimic his gestures, like the way he brushed the curl off his forehead with the back of his palm, or the way he half shrugged with his left shoulder when he was agreeing with something.

As far as Vee was concerned, he got two thumbs up as a male role model, at least in this setting. If Ben brought the boys along on a date, they'd see a whole different side of him…but that was hardly likely to happen. Besides, it was clear that Ben was careful to moderate his behavior so that he didn't say anything that might confuse the boys or set a bad example, which meant that he probably wouldn't let them anywhere near his social life.

A half hour later, they were back at the shop and Ben had unhooked her truck from the towline.

"You want me to see if I can take care of this now?" he asked, popping the hood and leaning in to get a closer look at the engine. "I can't promise I can make a quick fix. Most engine repairs take at least a couple of hours of labor time. Sometimes more like days, especially if we don't have the parts on hand."

She glanced at her watch and shook her head.

"No, that's okay," she affirmed. "I'm obviously going to have to change my plans, so there's no rush."

Not today, anyway. There was no point in trying to make it to Amarillo and back now, not with the sun already halfway down in the west. She'd have to make her excursion another day, and it would have to be soon. Not that she could count on having another free day between now and Saturday. She might have to come up with a Plan B or else rush into town and back, grabbing the first dress that caught her eye.

That's if she didn't completely lose her courage first and nix the whole idea.

At this point, that was a very big *if*.

Dear Veronica Jayne,
Today has been a good day. It always is when

I get to spend time with family and friends. I don't ever want to take that for granted. Remind me of that if I start complaining about life, will you? It's so easy to forget how many blessings God has showered me with.

I've got a super busy weekend, so I've been spending extra time on our project so I don't get behind. I'm organizing the final presentation with the software. I was blown over by how well your script and my graphics meshed together—better even than we'd planned. I think you'll be surprised when you see them. I'll attach the whole thing to an email once I'm sure I've got things the way I want them.

Excellent work on the script, by the way. The photos would be nothing without that great narration. I know I've said it before, but it bears repeating—I'm so happy you're my partner! Two thumbs up!

Sincerely,

BJ

Ben's gaze slid across the inner workings of Vee's truck, his years of working on engines making it easy for him to spot the problem.

"It looks like your timing belt snapped," he said, his hands gliding expertly over the engine's surface as he peered here and there to be certain he was making a complete diagnosis of the vehicle. "I'm afraid I'll have to special order some of the parts in order to fix it, so it may be a day or two before you get your truck back."

"You can't just slide on a new timing belt and call it good?" she asked hopefully.

He chuckled. "Not exactly. Let's just say that it's a little more complicated than that. I have to take the engine apart just to reach the area where I need to work. That's going to take some time in and of itself. Plus, with Serendipity being such a small town, off the beaten track and all, we don't keep a lot of spare parts at the shop. That would be too much of a burden on the shop's overhead. We've found that it's easier to order parts in when we have specific requests and know just what we need."

She sighed and smoothed her hair with her palm. "That figures. So what are we looking at? A week? Two weeks?"

"Well, hopefully it won't be quite that long." His gaze shifted briefly to where his nephews crouched, looking through a toolbox full of various-sized wrenches. "You need it for your work, right?"

"Exactly. Not to mention the special occasions coming up. Between the Easter banquet and Easter week services, my dance card is full to the brim. If it's going to be a long time, I may have to try to find some other reliable means of transportation to tide me over."

She groaned aloud. "And it'll be expensive, too, I'm guessing. A month's wages down the drain, right? Do I need to start looking for a third job?" She closed her eyes and raised her hands as if she were being held up by a gun-toting thief. "Just please make it a clean wound. That's all I can ask after the lovely day I've had."

He laughed. "You sound like a cup-half-empty kind of girl," he teased. "I don't want you worrying about time or money. It sounds like you've got enough on your plate as it is. I'll tell you what. How about if I cut you a break? I'll do the work on my own time and only charge you for the parts I use."

Her gaze locked on his, her almond-colored eyes narrowing. He'd never realized how beautiful they were until this moment. His stomach did a backflip as she stared him down. His throat bobbed as he tried to swallow.

"What?" he asked when she didn't speak.

"Why would you do this for me?" she asked suspiciously, her gaze narrowing on him.

Now *that* was a good question.

Why *would* he offer to help Vee? He'd done some really dumb things—like offering to work for free—early on in his dating days.

He'd given of himself and gotten nothing back in return, except more dead-end relationships.

But even if he hadn't learned his lesson in that department—not to give too much of himself for free when he stood the risk of being hurt—there was no overlooking one fact.

He and Vee weren't dating. She didn't even like him overmuch.

So what was he doing? And more to the point—why?

Why should he put himself out for her when she was very rarely even nice to him? Wouldn't he simply be laying himself out like a carpet and asking to be walked on?

When the silence dragged on, she apparently decided that he didn't have an answer to give, or at least not one that either of them would believe. Instead, she wandered to the other end of the garage and nonchalantly peeked under the vinyl cover of a hooded sports car.

His sports car, as it happened. Pride welled in his chest. This beauty was a classic Mustang rebuilt with his own two hands over a period of several months. He'd repainted her a deep navy blue with black trim, and she was custom-made from the engine to the wheel rims.

To say he was proud of that car would be an understatement. It was practically his baby. He'd spent countless hours nursing it to health and making her live up to the vision in his mind. But he'd never once, until now, showed her off to anyone other than his uncle. Even then, he'd only given Uncle Derek the merest glimpse of her. This was the first time he had considered showing her off for real, and his nerves crackled with tension.

"You're welcome to have a look," he said, carefully removing the cover on the shiny blue vehicle, which had been methodically waxed from stem to stern until it sparkled with a keen luster. The tire rims were gleamed silver and the black leather interior had been polished until it shone.

Vee whistled her appreciation and Ben stood up an inch taller, unable to still the smile growing on his face.

"Wow," she complimented, walking slowly around the vehicle, stopping to admire it from various vantage points. "Now *that* is a sports car. I've never seen anything quite so nice. It's really beautiful, Ben. Did you do the work yourself?"

Pride chased ego in dizzying circles in his stomach and curled up into his throat. He coughed into the crook of his shoulder.

"Who owns it? I'm so jealous, whoever they are. I've never seen anyone driving it around here, that's for sure. I would have remembered a car as fancy as that."

For some reason, her comments affected him more than he would have liked. He didn't know why it mattered what she thought. She probably didn't know a sports car from a Zamboni, but her smile was so genuine and her approval so apparent that he couldn't help the pride that welled in his chest.

It was an odd feeling. While there was no question that he was proud of his work on the car, there was something about the fact that it was specifically Vee Bishop's admiration that stroked his ego even more. That, he knew, ought to be cause for concern in itself, but he had to admit he liked the feeling.

"It's mine and I rebuilt her myself," he confirmed. "All the way from the ground up. She's my pet project. Between the auto shop and the fire station I haven't had much time to put into any kind of a hobby, so it's taken me several months to get her this far."

"She's definitely a beauty. You do good work."

"Thanks," he said, choking up again. He settled his weight on the balls of his feet. He was wound up like a top, waiting for her to spin him.

"So why haven't I seen you driving her around?"

"I suppose I was waiting until she was finished to show her off, until she was just perfect. I only drive her late at night when no one is around to see her while I get the engine in tip-top shape. I think she's close to making her debut now."

"I should say so. I'm impressed. I didn't know you rebuilt cars."

"Only this one." If she didn't stop escalating his ego, his chest was going to pop like an overinflated balloon. As it was, his adrenaline was running overtime, making his pulse buzz in his ears. "I suppose you could call rebuilding her my hobby, of sorts."

"Well, it definitely puts *my* hobby to shame."

"Really? What do you do for fun?" He was genuinely curious, although he couldn't have explained why. Maybe it was that she'd shown so much interest in what he'd done that he felt he ought to reciprocate.

She laughed, looking a little self-conscious, which wasn't like Vee at all. At least, not the Vee Ben knew—the woman who was always in control, who always knew what to do or say in any given situation. The woman who was generally as strung up as tight as a bow.

And the woman who didn't like *him* at *all*.

Or at least he didn't think she did. She didn't usually treat him with the respect she was showing him now, and that put her in a new light for him.

Maybe he was judging her too harshly, based mostly on her outward appearance and attitude. Yes, she sported a tight bun and an even tighter expression, but he supposed that was understandable given her circumstances. She worked in a tough, nearly exclusively male environment at the fire station. Maybe she wasn't as rigid as he'd been given to believe she was.

"Candles. I make candles," she said, shattering whatever preconceived notions Ben had had of her. "You know the ones on the end cap in the craft section of Emerson's? Those would be mine." She snorted. "Pathetic, I know."

Now it was Ben's turn to whistle his surprise.

Landscaping. Candle making. Firefighting. What else did he not know about her?

Vee was a complete enigma. She surprised him at every turn. Whatever else he thought of her, he didn't consider her pathetic in any way, shape or form.

"Not at all," he said aloud. "I bought some of those candles for my mama last Christmas. She loves them. She lights them whenever she takes a bubble bath, and she won't even consider using any others."

Vee murmured something Ben didn't quite pick up, but before he could figure it out, his attention was drawn to his two antsy nephews. They'd been cooped up in the truck too long and they were raring to do something physical.

"Uncle Ben!" Felix shouted from the far corner of the shop. "Can you put us up on the lift?"

"Please?" little Nigel pleaded.

Ben laughed. "Okay, guys, but just this once. We need to get Miss Bishop back to her house. I'm sure she doesn't want to hang around this greasy old garage all day."

"Oh, no, I—" Vee started to protest but then dropped silent, watching as Ben situated the boys on the hydraulic lift, which was generally used to raise cars off the ground so he could work underneath them.

After making sure the boys' feet were safely away from the edges, he moved to the electrical box and flipped a switch. The lift ground to life and the boys squealed in glee.

"Ben!" Vee exclaimed in dismay. She rushed to his side and reached for his elbow before she'd even finished saying his name. "Surely you're not going to—"

"Let the boys take a little ride up the lift? Why not? My uncle used to allow me to take a jaunt up there all the time, and no harm ever came to me. Don't worry. It's fun. Nothing to be concerned about. Besides, my nephews have done this before. Plenty of times."

"That doesn't make it safe." Now she was starting to sound like the woman he knew—the one who had an opinion on everything—an opinion that usually said that whatever he did was wrong. Vee Bishop pushed her weight around, tiny as she was, and always thought she needed to micromanage every tiny detail of what was going on around her.

"Maybe you're not aware of this fact, but boys like to have a little danger in their lives," he said. He was still smiling, but it was starting to feel forced now. "Not, of course, that I'm suggesting that riding the lift is really dangerous. It's not. Believe me, I've got it completely under control. I promise I won't go an inch higher than five feet. Felix and Nigel climb trees taller than that."

"With cement underneath them?" Vee stepped back, but she didn't look happy about it. She folded her arms in front of her and scowled at him. "If they get hurt it's on you."

Of course it was on him. He was in charge of his nephews for the day. He wouldn't let them do anything truly dangerous. They wouldn't get hurt on his watch.

"We'll take you home as soon as we're done here," he said, grinning when his nephews shrieked with delight at being carried up by the rising lift.

"If we don't have to go to the hospital first," she grumbled under her breath.

He spared her an exasperated glance. Really? Did she not trust him at *all?*

"Fine," she conceded as she met his gaze. "Could you drop me by my father's house instead? He didn't sound at his best when I talked to him earlier, and I just want to make sure he's all right. I can get Eli to take me home after he finishes his shift at the police station."

"Sure thing," Ben assured her.

"If it's an inconvenience I can—"

He didn't let her finish. "It's not an inconvenience. Okay, boys. Get your balance and watch where you're standing. I'm going to take you down now."

The boys groaned in unison, but they followed Ben's directions and situated themselves safely on the lift before Ben brought it down.

Slowly. Carefully.

The whole thing had been perfectly harmless, just as he'd said.

"See?" He flashed Vee a satisfied, and possibly a bit triumphant, smile. "All safe and sound."

Vee shrugged, still appearing unconvinced. Ben pushed back the wave of irritation he felt at the way she wouldn't back down, even now that he'd been proved right. Why couldn't she believe in him, even a little? Why did she always assume the worst when he was involved?

Resolutely, he turned away from her, focusing on the boys. He wasn't going to let Vee spoil the pleasure he felt from spending time with them.

If Vee Bishop wanted to disapprove of him, fine. He wasn't going to let it bother him one single bit.

Chapter Six

Dear BJ,

Today didn't go as planned, but days seldom do, do they? In my experience, God doesn't always have the same agenda I do. It's more than rolling with the punches. It's adapting— trying to see what God wants me to learn.

Sometimes I feel that I hinder myself. My own personal perception of events skews my actions, and often I wonder whether or not I'm walking the right road. I question if I'm doing the correct things at all—taking this Spanish class, moving forward with my life, into mission work.

That's when I have to trust God the most, I guess—and lean on friends like you. Thank you for letting me vent.

In Christ,

Veronica Jayne

Vee couldn't believe Ben had allowed his nephews to ride on the hydraulic lift, even if he had only raised them a few feet in the air. She could not imagine what he was thinking, but she'd been around her own brothers long enough to know that guys often took irrational risks for no apparent reason. It appeared to be in their DNA, passed on from generation to generation.

Like uncle to nephews, for example.

"Would you like to come in for a moment?" she asked as Ben pulled his truck into her father's long, washboard dirt driveway. "I'm sure he'd be glad to have the company, especially the boys. Children always make him smile."

She could only hope that was true. It used to be, but now it was hard to say *what,* if anything, would make her father smile. Her dad didn't find joy in much since his wife's death. He rarely left the house, preferring to sit by the fire with one of his books. He didn't even attend regular Sunday services at the church anymore.

It was a matter of constant prayer for Vee. She didn't know what to do for him or how to reach him, and neither did her brothers.

No matter what they tried, from family dinners to community gatherings, nothing seemed to help. In fact, he seemed to be withdrawing more and more into his shell with each passing day. Vee worried about his health, which appeared to be declining. Where once there was a strong, robust man heading the Bishop clan, there was now a weary, world-worn soul. It broke Vee's heart every time she thought of him.

"You sure he won't mind having the boys around?" Ben reiterated. "They're pretty wound up right now, and I know your father hasn't been feeling well lately."

Vee chuckled. "Believe me, he's used to rowdy boys," she said. "Don't forget, he raised Cole and Eli."

Boys didn't get any rowdier than Cole and Eli. Even as adults her brothers tended to be loud and raucous.

What she didn't say was that she wasn't positive how he'd handle it now. The boys might brighten his day. Hopefully. Otherwise, they'd simply tire him out and send him further into seclusion.

It was a chance she had to take. She would do anything to break her father out of his shell and put him back on the road to healing. She knew as well as her father that grief was inevitable. It was what a person did with it that counted in the long run.

"Just for a moment, then," Ben agreed. "I've noticed that your father hasn't been to Sunday services at church for a few weeks, and I'd like the opportunity to say hello and see how he's faring."

"Dad?" she called, knocking twice before entering the house where she'd grown up. "I have a surprise for you!"

"You know I don't like surprises," her dad growled, his voice as scratchy as the scruff on his chin. Although it was well into the afternoon, her father shuffled into the living room still dressed in his ragged blue bathrobe and worn-out slippers. Vee was embarrassed for him but not about him. Anyone with eyes could see he was still grieving.

He walked hunched over like a man twenty years past his age. His short gray hair was ruffled and his brown eyes cloudy—at least until he saw Felix and Nigel.

"Hey, boys," he exclaimed, smoothing his hair back with his fingers as if that would somehow make him more presentable. "Tell me, who do we have here?"

Ben made the introductions. "These are my sister's kids, Felix and Nigel."

"Kayla's boys. Well, I'll be a rooster's uncle. Just let me put on another pot of coffee," her father said as they all moved into the kitchen.

"I'll get it." Vee was relieved to have something to do with her hands, though making coffee didn't keep her mind as occupied as she would have liked. Her heart shattered every time she saw her father this way. She felt so helpless. All she could do was pray, and as she scooped grounds into the filter, she silently did just that. At least seeing Felix and Nigel had seemed to have a positive effect on the man.

"I'll bet you boys don't want to sit around the table while the adults chitter-chatter, now, do you?"

The boys' combined protest was enough to convince every adult in the room that they did not want to be holed up in a house with a bunch of boring adults. Vee chuckled at their enthusiasm.

"I've got a big backyard just right for children," her father continued. "My own three kids used to play out back all the time. It was all their mother and I could do to keep those three out of trouble. They were always fighting with each other, falling out of trees, scraping their knees on the pavement…"

Her father's expression took on a distant quality, and for a moment Vee wondered if he even knew where he was, much less that his own daughter was in the room and that she, along with her brothers, were all grown up now. His mental status seemed to be declining with every passing day.

Then, just as quickly as he'd faded out, her

father's face brightened and he returned to the present. It was almost frightening how easily she could see the transformation in his gaze.

"Now, somewhere around this old house," he said, tapping his index finger on his chin, "I've got a ball for you boys to play with. Hmm. I wonder where I put it?"

His bushy gray eyebrows lowered over his nose as he paused, concentrating. After a moment he grunted and nodded to himself, then rose from his chair with a groan and scuttled out to the front hall closet. *Scuttled* was precisely the right word for the way he moved. He reminded Vee of a crab she'd once seen on a beach when she'd visited the Oregon coast.

The top half of her father's body disappeared into the closet as he fished through the coats, and she heard his muffled shout of triumph and delight when he finally found his prize.

"Here we are, boys," he called out, lofting a black-and-white checkered soccer ball at Felix, who caught it easily and without hesitation. The ball must have been the one that belonged to Vee and her brothers way back when. She couldn't imagine why her parents would have kept it all these years, but it certainly came in handy now.

"C'mon, Nigel. Race you to the back!" Felix took off at a sprint.

"No fair," Nigel squealed, darting off after his brother. "You got a head start."

Her father laughed. Actually *laughed*.

Vee didn't think she'd heard that happy sound since before her mother's funeral. A little glow of hope, like the flicker of a candle, warmed her heart, and she offered a quick, silent prayer of gratitude to God for allowing her to witness the moment. Just now, thanks to Felix and Nigel, she'd been given just the tiniest glimpse of hope that her father might finally begin to settle his grief and move on with his life.

Maybe not right away, but Vee prayed it would be soon. Seeing her father with the boys was a good first step. It's what her mother would have wanted.

Vee poured coffee into three mugs and settled at the kitchen table with Ben and her father. Ben immediately swept her father into conversation, telling him about her truck repairs, bringing him up to date with all the goings-on around town and filling him in on the topic of Pastor Shawn's new series of sermons.

Ben was so laid-back and friendly that it didn't take long for him to put her father at ease. It was a good thing, too, because even with today's monumental progress, Vee was never quite sure what to say to her father these days. She was thankful she didn't have to carry the

conversation by herself. She was always afraid
she'd say something that would upset him or,
worse yet, accidentally mention her mother and
send him even deeper into his shell.

Ben might look like a tough guy on the outside, but Vee had to admit he had a sensitive
side. He was kind and gentle to her father without being condescending. It was eye-opening for
her to see this side of a man who would reach
out to an older neighbor in his time of need.

He was sweet. And perceptive. Almost like
BJ.

Vee's throat closed and she almost choked
on her sip of coffee. Ben was definitely nothing like BJ.

Or at least, as much as she knew about BJ.
The realization struck her that BJ was nothing
more than words on a computer screen. She
had a sense of his personality, and he'd told her
about his goals and dreams, but she knew so
little about the day-to-day aspects of his life.
Did he have nephews, like Ben, who he enjoyed
spending time with? Was he a good neighbor,
a good friend, to the people he saw every day?

Ben, however—*Ben* was very much a real
man. She could see him, hear him, even touch
those enormous biceps of his if she was so inclined.

She coughed, trying to force air back into her

lungs, but it didn't seem to help. Ben couldn't possibly be half the man BJ was, nor would he ever be. She jammed that frequency of thinking before it could be broadcast any further.

Of course she was thankful for Ben's help. He'd been there to rescue her earlier, with his big old tow truck and amiable half grin. And now he was being nice to her father, which was a big plus in her book.

But the feelings she was experiencing—those couldn't be more than mismatched forms of gratitude, could they? She didn't even like Ben, but at this exact moment, she had to actively remind herself why she disliked him.

He might be acting nice today, but not all that long ago he'd broken her best friend's heart. How could Vee possibly put that aside, even for a moment?

BJ wasn't like that. That was good enough for her.

Or was it?

Her heart stuck in her throat and she almost choked again. What if she was using her quasi-relationship with a cyber-guy to avoid dealing with the real thing?

In some ways, wasn't that exactly what her father was doing? Avoiding reality to shield him from his own grief? She thought back to when she'd first been paired with BJ in her Spanish class, and a shiver passed through her when she realized that their friendship had started up just after her mother's passing.

Yes, BJ was a real person, and she'd connected with him in a very real way…but it probably wasn't a coincidence that she'd thrown herself into getting to know him right at that time rather than reaching out to the people in town.

Her chest felt suddenly heavy with sorrow, another sniper-strike of grief aimed straight at her heart when she wasn't looking.

Was it like that for her father, too? Her mother had been the love of his life. No wonder he couldn't cope.

Vee got up from the table and stared out the kitchen window, watching the boys laughing and talking as they kicked the soccer ball back and forth to each other. She'd had so many good times in that backyard that she could hardly remember them all. Swinging bats and kicking balls with Cole and Eli. Playing cops and robbers and tag and hide-and-seek from the moment the sun rose in the sky until their mother forced them inside at dusk.

What had happened to that innocent feeling she'd had as a child? When had she become so jaded about life?

She recalled how once she'd followed her brothers up the big, spreading oak in the middle of the yard. They'd been trying to get away from her, their pesky little sister, and Eli had climbed too high, trying to balance on a branch that couldn't support his weight.

He'd fallen fifteen feet and had broken an arm and twisted an ankle. She remembered how frightened she'd been to watch paramedics taking him away on a stretcher, thinking it was her fault and that her brother might not come home from the hospital.

She always had been a little melodramatic about that sort of thing. No wonder she'd panicked when Ben had allowed his nephews to ride up the hydraulic lift. Could anyone blame her for being a little overcautious? But it was one thing to be wary of physical dangers—and it was another thing entirely to be cautious about opening her heart to the people around her.

When had she closed herself down to the outside world, like her father was doing now? She hadn't always approached personal relationships with an abundance of prudence and few expectations.

She turned back to her father, who was chuckling at some story that Ben was regaling

him with. Ben's attention was definitely helping her father to come out of his shell of misery and grief.

Maybe it was time for Vee to do the same thing.

Chapter Seven

Dear BJ,

I know I just sent you another email a little while ago. I hope you don't feel like I'm inundating your inbox with messages, but I think I've had another revelation about myself, and I wanted to share it with you. You understand me better than anyone else I know, next to God, of course.

I won't bore you with the details, but suffice it to say that after today, I'm going to be making some major changes in my life. I never realized until now that the woman I see when I glimpse at my reflection in the mirror every morning may not be the person others see when they look at me. We've been talking a lot about change, but maybe it's not change at all so much as just reconciling what's on the inside of me with what people see when they look at me.

Anyway, that isn't the only reason I'm emailing you tonight. I wanted to double-check with you to make sure you didn't need anything else from me for our project.

Sincerely,
Veronica Jayne

It had taken Vee an hour to curl her hair into the soft ringlets that now framed her face.

An *hour!*

How so many women did this on a daily basis was beyond her comprehension. Why would any woman put herself through such utter nonsense if she didn't have to? Vee didn't have the patience for this kind of self-torment, not even on her best day. And as long as it had taken her just to *curl her hair,* she wasn't certain this was going to be anything remotely resembling her *best* day.

Even so, she did have to admit to a fairly significant physical transformation. She stared into the mirror and saw someone she barely recognized. She'd brushed the sides of her long, flowing brown hair forward across her shoulders and allowed the rest to stream in waves down her back. She'd carefully lined and shaded her almond-colored eyes with sparkling silver eye shadow the way Olivia had taught her. She snorted at her reflection. She was a caricature of her normal makeup-less self, and she wasn't the least bit confident that she didn't look as silly as she felt.

This was crazy. It usually took her all of two minutes to pull her hair back in a knot and shun everything but the barest mineral foundation on her skin.

And as for plucking her eyebrows—what kind of barbarous personality had invented *that* particular brand of torture? She would rather relive Hazing Week at the fire academy than go through tweezing again, hair by painful hair, until her whole forehead was inflamed and burning red.

She shook her head at her reflection and scoffed. This whole idea was a big mistake from start to finish.

And she'd barely started what was sure to be an excruciatingly long day.

She was *so* tempted to undo all of the progress she'd made on herself, if a person could really call what she'd done to herself *progress*. A still-small inner voice was telling her to quit while she was ahead. The problem was that she was already late for setting up the Easter Banquet and she didn't want to miss another moment of it. Washing the makeup off her face and the curl out of her hair would take time she didn't have.

If she didn't hurry, she wouldn't be able to help with the meal at all. It was her first time serving with the fire department, although she, along with everyone else in Serendipity, had been involved with town fundraising for the event since she was in elementary school. The school held car washes and bake sales every year to help buy supplies for the dinner.

This time she'd be right in the middle of the action—actually physically helping the less fortunate—if she stopped staring at herself in the mirror and hightailed it to the community center.

She left the house without another glance. Less than ten minutes later she pulled her truck into the parking lot of the community center that served as the hub of many of Serendipity's social events. Thankfully, Ben had been able to secure the parts needed to fix her timing belt and had repaired her truck in time for her to drive it to the banquet.

Under normal circumstances she would have elected to walk the short distance from her apartment to the center, especially as nice a day as it was, but there was no *way* she was going to walk that far in heels.

In fact, walking at *all* was somewhat of an

issue. She'd always considered herself athletic and coordinated, but no matter how many times she practiced walking back and forth across her small apartment in three-inch heels, she could not seem to master the teetering-on-the-edge-of-falling feeling those ridiculous shoes produced.

Another "how do they do it" moment. She had a new appreciation for the women who attempted to wear heels on a daily basis.

Score one for the ladies of high fashion.

She'd almost reached the front door of the community center and was about to call out a greeting to a couple of her brother's cop friends who were lounging by the door, but they spied her first before she could get a single word out.

One of the guys, Brody, had been stretched back on a metal bench, his arm extended over the back. His friend Slade had been standing with one foot on the bench, leaning forward with his forearm on his knee for balance. They'd appeared deep in conversation, at least until Vee strolled up, though maybe *stroll* was too generous a word for the actual gait she was using.

More like *lumbering* or *teetering*.

Just not, hopefully, if God was gracious to her, *falling on her face*.

Before she could so much as say hello to the

guys, both of the men sprang to their feet like twin Jack-in-the-boxes after the trap mechanisms had been dispatched.

"Let me get that door for you," said Brody, who had sprinted over to the set of steel double doors and had thus reached them first. He opened the right door with a flourish and waved for her to go through.

"No, allow me." Slade reached for the opposite door, but when he tugged, it didn't open. He grimaced and a bright-red flush rose to his face, but he recovered quickly.

"At least let me escort you in," he crooned with what Vee presumed he must think was his best swaggering grin. To Vee it looked more like a laughably cocky contortion, which was made even more entertaining by the fact that he crooked his arm and offered his elbow to escort her like they were in a scene in an old movie.

Who were these fools, and what had they done with the police squadron?

"Thanks, guys, but I think I can manage on my own." She probably was being overoptimistic, given the circumstances, but whether she wanted to admit it or not, she was flustered by the way the men were acting. They'd certainly never offered to open a door for her before, much less presented an arm for her to take.

What was up with that?

And then it struck her like a lightning bolt out of the blue.

Zap!

They didn't recognize her.

At least, they hadn't known who she was until she spoke to them. When they heard her voice, the men turned as one, astonishment written on both of their faces, their eyes widening and their jaws dropping.

"Vee?" Brody queried, his tone a mixture of bemusement and disbelief. Mostly disbelief.

"Well, I never," Slade muttered under his breath, following the statement with a low wolf whistle as his gaze followed her figure from her eyes all the way to her toes, and then back up again.

Vee lifted her chin. "What is your problem?"

She should have been ready for this. She squared her shoulders. She *was* ready for this.

The looks on these guys' faces was pretty much the reaction she'd expected from people—at least the part where they stared at her in shock. Frankly, she'd expected that to happen the second they caught sight of her. She couldn't believe that she'd managed to change her outward appearance so much that not only had the guys not recognized her when she'd first arrived, but her appearance had sent them scurrying to one-up each other.

Oh, well. She didn't have time to waste on a couple of knuckleheads like Brody and Slade. She perused the room, trying to find Chief Jenkins. As was town tradition, he and the police chief were responsible for handing out orders and work details to the people under their respective commands.

Instead of finding Chief Jenkins, her eyes met and locked with Ben Atwood's. And unlike the fellows at the door, she was immediately and startlingly aware that *he* knew exactly who she was. There wasn't a moment's doubt or hesitation in his eyes, though he looked at least as stunned as Brody and Slade had been.

Her heart jumped into her throat at the sheer admiration in his eyes. For some reason, that one moment almost made the whole tortuous episode seem worth it.

But only for a second—before someone bumped into her from behind, jarring her enough for her to belatedly come to her senses.

This was *Ben Atwood* who had her heart racing.

How could that be?

Ben was certain his jaw dropped. Even if he'd managed a slick recovery, the astonishment he was feeling in every pore of his being must have been written all over his face.

Who was this vision of loveliness floating across the room at him? His brain was spinning so fast he was sure his eyes must be deceiving him.

No one needed to tell him that it was *Vee* in that gorgeous royal-blue dress. He was perfectly, maddeningly aware it was her. And technically, she was limping, not floating.

But *wow*.

Wow. Wow. *Wow*.

The last time he'd seen her, he'd been rescuing her from her broken-down vehicle. She'd been wearing ratty jeans and a ragged T-shirt, and her forehead had been smeared with grease. She'd looked fresh and innocent and mischievous. It suited her.

But today, she'd cleaned up like...well, like a princess. There was no other way to describe her. He'd had no idea that the thick brown hair she kept so tightly pulled back in a knot at the back of her head could be the long, curly hair that was now cascading down around her shoulders and streaming three-quarters of the way down her back. He'd known that her eyes were beautiful and distinctive, but now they were enhanced by sparkly gray eye shadow and a subtle arch to her brows that called him to her gaze.

If it weren't for the frown lining her face, the

transformation from duckling to swan would have been complete.

Not that he'd ever thought of Vee as ugly. Stern, maybe, but not unattractive.

Now she was stunning. He couldn't seem to tear his gaze away from her in her dazzling dress and the high heels that accentuated her lean, womanly figure and surprisingly long legs for a person of her stature. He would never have imagined that under the tiny, no-nonsense attitude was a woman who would turn heads at even the most regal of functions, much less at a simple town banquet.

And there was no doubt that she *was* turning heads. Oh, yes indeed she was.

Men and women alike had stopped what they were doing to gaze at the newcomer in their midst. Observing the crowd, Ben could clearly see that Vee's change in appearance had done a number on them. Vee had known these folks all of her life, but it was obvious that it took most of them a minute to realize it was Vee Bishop under that perfectly flowing hair and dazzling makeup.

For some reason Ben hadn't been in doubt at all. She'd thrown him for a loop, but not that way.

It wasn't long before the whole room was abuzz, with everyone noisily wondering the hows and whys of Vee's transformation. Three of Vee's single girlfriends—cheerfully christened throughout the town as the Little Chicks because of their tendency to speak in high, twittering tones—hovered around Vee, talking over themselves in their excitement to be heard. The moniker Little Chicks fit them—it definitely sounded like chirping to Ben.

And taking the spot closest to Vee was her best friend—who also happened to be one of Ben's ex-girlfriends. Olivia Tate. Jo Spencer appeared at Vee's other side and looped their arms together, exclaiming about how beautiful she looked loudly enough for the entire room to hear.

The women had rallied around Vee quickly, despite the fact that she was beyond a doubt the most beautiful woman in the room. There was no jealousy or pettiness. All of the girls were supporting her—not that Vee had ever needed any kind of support in the past.

Ben knew that moving into that particular circle, a flock of protective women nurturing their own, would be hazardous to any man's health, especially him with his history with Olivia. Even the other guys appeared to be taking their time to watch rather than approach.

Their loss.

Ben bucked up his nerves, swallowed his

amazement and darted forward, taking Vee's other arm before another man could lay claim to it. Olivia moved to the side, allowing him more room in their circle.

As soon as he touched Vee, her deer-in-the-headlights expression disappeared, replaced by a hard-as-nails determination that was completely at odds with the soft ebb and flow of her gown.

"You look just lovely, dear," Jo said, patting Vee's arm. "Doesn't she, Ben?"

"Yeah," he agreed, but the word came out an octave lower than his usual voice and had an odd, husky tone to it. Discomfited, he cleared his throat. It figured that Jo would aim her question directly toward him when he was having a hard time finding his voice.

He felt like he should say more than simply assenting to Jo's comment, but his mind was so jumbled he couldn't think coherently. What had happened to his brain?

After a long, painful pause, he continued. "You look nice, Vee."

Which was the understatement of the century. Idiot. What was he thinking?

He *wasn't* thinking. That was the problem. He felt like hitting himself in the head to restore some mental function.

"Has anyone seen Chief around?" Vee asked, scanning the room and clearly determining to ignore the blatant admiration she was receiving. "I've got to get my orders so I can get busy helping out around here. No sense standing around doing nothing when I can be working."

"Are you kidding me?" Ben blurted before he thought better of it. Unfortunately, his statement was not only foolish—it was loud.

Every woman within hearing distance narrowed their eyes on him. He shrugged uncomfortably.

"I just meant that I wouldn't want Vee to get her dress dirty," he stated defensively. "It's so pretty. I'd hate for her to ruin it serving food."

"I didn't ask your opinion," Vee retorted, her tone icy. "And I didn't come here to stand around gawking, which is what everyone else appears to be doing. This is my first year with the fire department and I'm not about to miss the opportunity to help."

Ouch. Well, that was a slap in the face and probably well-deserved.

Vee might look like a different woman on the outside, but her attitude hadn't changed a bit. Same old tough-as-nails Vee, with a chip on her shoulder the size of a boulder and an attitude to match.

"Of course you're going to be helping," Jo assured Vee in a conciliatory voice, patting her arm for reassurance. "Look, there—I see Chief now."

As a matter of fact, Chief Jenkins was at that moment making his way through the crowd, his astonished gaze on Vee as he moved forward. And even more surprising—Vee's *father* was with him.

"Daddy!" she exclaimed, running up to hug him and plant a kiss on his freshly shaved cheek. "What on earth are you doing here?"

Her father barked out a husky laugh. "The same thing you're doing, I imagine. I offered to put my cooking skills to good use, and I've only just now had a break from the kitchen. I've been cooking since six this morning. Believe me, those church ladies can be real slave drivers when they want to be."

Vee laughed and hugged him again. Ben could see the sheer joy shining from her eyes. He knew how concerned she'd been over the way her father had holed himself up in his house after the death of his wife.

It was great to see him out and about, and it was even better to see the beautiful smile of delight on Vee's face.

"If I may say so, you look absolutely gorgeous,

my dear," Chief said when he reached Vee. "Truly stunning."

Vee's smile widened even more at Chief's compliment. If Ben wasn't mistaken, she even blushed.

Vee Bishop. Blushing at a compliment.

Would wonders never cease.

"Thank you, Chief," Vee responded in a lilting tone much lighter than her usual rich alto, but a moment later she was back to her no-nonsense self. "Reporting for duty, sir. Where do you want me?"

Chief's bushy gray eyebrows lifted in surprise. "Goodness, Vee, I wouldn't have expected that you'd want to get your hands dirty, not with your fancy dress and all."

She leveled him with a glare. Ben would not have wanted to be Chief at that moment.

Even though Chief Jenkins was used to being in charge, he actually winced.

"Maybe you could greet people at the door?" he suggested weakly.

Ha! Ben wanted to crow. See? He wasn't the only one who thought Vee's getup wasn't appropriate for a worker bee at a messy banquet dinner.

Vee sighed, clearly frustrated. "What is it with you guys? I came to work, not to watch.

What's the problem? Do you want me to run back home and change?"

No, Ben did *not* want her to change—but he had the sense to keep his mouth shut. It would be a shame to see Vee walk out of the community center now and come back dressed in her usual attire of jeans and a cotton shirt. Truly. A real shame.

"I *am* going to help out with the Easter banquet," she continued obstinately.

"Which she is perfectly capable of doing in a dress," Jo added.

Chief's gaze turned to Jo and he immediately nodded his consent. People didn't often cross Jo Spencer, and it didn't look like Chief was going to do so now. Besides, it was very likely that if he argued, he'd find himself ganged up on by a whole horde of women, not just Jo, and no man wanted to be put in that position, not even the chief of the fire station.

"Yes, of course," he offered. "I'm sure we can find you something to do."

Something *appropriate,* Ben hoped.

"I was just going to see if I could help set up tables," Ben said, addressing Vee. "Maybe you could follow along with plates and silverware?" He held his breath, waiting to see if she was going to blow up at him or not.

Surprisingly, she looked relieved at his suggestion. "Sure. I guess I can do that. Then maybe I can help serve the food."

Ben nodded. Obviously it wouldn't do any good to argue with her. The harder any of them pushed, the harder she'd push back.

Maybe he could discreetly lead her into the least messy projects. She didn't have to know he was moving with any particular purpose in mind or that he was keeping a close eye on her.

It was a personal thing.

Because how sad would it be if she got that pretty blue dress dirty? That would be a disservice to all of mankind.

He had to admit that he himself couldn't stop staring at her and reveling in the remarkable change she had made. If he had to work by her side all afternoon to make sure she didn't get food slopped all over her, or if he had to take care of cleaning all the greasy pans himself so she didn't have to, then so be it.

A man had to do what a man had to do.

Chapter Eight

By the time Vee had finished serving hot biscuits during the banquet and had washed down all of the tablecloths with a wet rag afterward, she was nearly ready to call a forfeit to the game.

Not only was she utterly exhausted, but her feet felt as if they'd been in a vise for a week. She was certain she had several blisters forming, and all she could think about was going home to soak her aching toes in a hot bath with fragrant candles and lots of bubbles to soothe her frayed nerves.

She couldn't wait to write to BJ and tell him how the event had gone…the *event* in question being the unveiling of her new look rather than the Easter banquet itself. The truth was, both affairs were a surprising success after everyone got used to the idea that she was wearing a dress and stopped harassing her about it. Even after everyone had turned to their work, she'd notice men's eyes on her from time to time.

Men. Watching her. Simply mind-boggling.

Vee put a hand to the small of her back and stretched. It was all she could do to keep from groaning aloud, but because Ben had not left her side since the beginning of the afternoon, pride meant that she had to keep her aches and pains to herself, even if that meant gritting her teeth until her jaw hurt.

She wasn't about to admit that the dress or the heels in any way fazed her or made her life more difficult. She'd toughed out more agonizingly painful situations than the high heels that were biting into her feet. Hazing Week at the fire academy had been worse.

Hadn't it? At the moment, she couldn't think of anything she'd experienced that hurt worse than the way that her shoes were cutting off the circulation in her feet.

But she could do it. It was mind over matter—at least until she was able get away from the banquet and tear the nasty, tortuous heels from her feet.

She glanced up to see Ben staring at her speculatively, but he looked away as soon as their eyes met.

"What?" she asked, feeling uncomfortable

with his overt perusal. Had he realized the direction her thoughts were going? Had her feelings shown on her face?

Ugh. How was she going to explain that?

Ben flashed a half smile and shook his head. "It's nothing."

She shrugged. "Suit yourself."

"But you do look especially pretty today, just so you know," he continued, as if he hadn't just the very moment before told her he didn't have anything to say.

Especially?

Did that mean he thought she was at least sort of pretty *all* of the time? No one had ever called her pretty before, at least not anyone besides her father and mother, and on the odd occasion, her brothers, and now she was hearing it from virtually everyone around her.

It was not only groundbreaking—it was earth-shattering. Yet somehow Ben's remark held more weight with her, more even than all the other compliments combined.

Which was utterly ridiculous, and she needed to stop that little ego-flattering train of thought right now, before it pulled out of the station.

She should know better than to be affected by transient smooth talk just because those types of words had never before been directed her way, especially by a man. Those sweet yet dubious words were coming from the mouth of a man who'd had an endless string of dates on his arm. He'd probably fed that very same line to half of the single women in Serendipity.

After all, he'd dated most of them at one time or another since he'd returned to town from serving in the National Guard. But no matter what she told herself, heat rose to her face nonetheless, and she knew her cheeks were stained a scorching red.

"Thank you," she said after a long pause. She thought she ought to at least acknowledge the compliment, even if it came from the biggest player in town. "And look here—I didn't even manage to get a single smudge of food on my dress," she continued drolly.

It could have been a teasing remark. The circumstances were ripe for a little flirtation. But somehow she'd managed to make it sound catty.

"Sorry," she apologized with a wince. She might have a million reasons to dislike and distrust Ben, but he hadn't done anything on this particular afternoon to warrant her verbal abuse. He'd been very kind to her and had kept her company all day. He'd even been nice to Olivia. It was probably just for show, but it was a start, or at least it might be.

Ben's smile was as genuine as his starlit bronze-green gaze. "Why are you sorry? In my opinion, you have every right to be defensive. Folks sure acted differently toward you today, didn't they?"

"You think?" There was *catty* again. She might as well have hissed. Rrreer! Fffft!

She took a deep breath and tried again. "I'm surprised you noticed."

She didn't mention that Ben had acted just as *differently* as the rest of them. Maybe more so. Not so blatant or so noticeable, maybe, but different just the same. He'd certainly never gone out of his way to spend that much time with her before.

"It was hard not to see it," he answered. "The guys from the fire station practically fell all over themselves trying to stand next to you in the serving line. And I don't want to think about how the dolts from the police force were acting toward you."

"And yet you won out."

His eyebrows danced. "I'm bigger."

Well, that was true.

"And I hope my motives were better," he added.

This time it was her eyebrows that jumped. Ben Atwood with good intentions? Now that was a laugh.

"How so?"

"Oh, come on, Vee. You have to have realized that after your appearance today, you're going to have dates lined up for the next year at least. You've been hiding yourself behind that firefighter's uniform and nobody knew the truth about just how pretty you really are. Are you trying to tell me that not one single man in the room approached you to ask you out? Don't bother because I won't believe you."

The heat roasting her face rose a few degrees higher. Was it getting hot in here or what?

Because the truth was, Ben was right. To her very great astonishment, a couple of local single men *had* asked for her phone number—not that she'd given it to them. If they wanted to call her, her number was listed in the phone book, the same as it had always been. Besides...

"That wasn't my intention at all," she assured him, wondering why she suddenly felt the over-powering need to explain herself to a man she didn't even like.

"Wasn't it?" The bronze in his eyes sparkled, dancing with the green.

She tossed a wadded-up paper napkin at him. "No, it was not," she stated, emphasizing each word. "I had something to prove to *myself* today. Not to anyone else. Especially not to a bunch of fickle men." Today men had asked for her phone number. Tomorrow, when she was back in her usual clothes, they wouldn't give her the time of day. Things would be back to the way they'd always been, with dull, boring Vee not turning *anyone's* head.

"And did you?" he queried, tilting his head. "Prove something to yourself?"

"In some ways I suppose I did," she admitted, chewing thoughtfully on her bottom lip. "I clarified some things, anyway."

"So you had fun?"

"Definitely. At least for part of the time. I really enjoyed serving the dinner—knowing that I was helping people in such a direct way. That was an incredible blessing, not only to them, but to me and our team. Still…"

"Still?" he echoed when she didn't immediately finish her statement.

She paused and frowned pensively. "You know what bothers me most about today?"

He shook his head. "No. What?"

"What you said earlier—your observation about how folks reacted to me today. I don't understand why people treated me differently just because I was wearing a dress. Something is off with that, don't you think?"

If his stunned gaze was anything to go by, she would have to guess that her statement took Ben aback. She was surprised when he agreed with her.

"Yeah, Vee. I do."

Dear Veronica Jayne,

Did you receive the introductory packet from the Sacred Heart Mission yet? I got mine in the mail yesterday. If you ask me, it looks pretty complicated. There are tons of forms to fill out, and we have to take a psychological assessment. Oh, and of course we have to have a complete physical workup with our primary care provider. I'm not worried about that part, though. I'm in pretty good shape—at least physically. The psychological part remains to be seen, ha ha.

I'm planning to start doing all the paperwork on my next day off. I want to send it in as soon as possible, especially because there's a very short window between now and summer orientation. I know you are just as anxious as I am to get out onto the mission field, and I'll be so happy to finally meet you in person if the Lord leads us to the same mission. What a great day that will be, huh?

I've been praying for you. I know you said you're going through a rough patch right now. All I can say is that I've been corresponding with you long enough to know you're a good person at heart.

Be brave. Step out of your comfort zone. Put yourself out there. But be gentle on yourself, too. I've said it before and I'll say it again.

I don't need to see your face to know what a special person you are. Even your thoughts are beautiful.

Yours,

BJ

Ben gritted his teeth as he strained to brace his palms against the weight bar and push his arms straight over his chest. He was bench-pressing two hundred pounds today, a good ten more than usual, pushing himself to the outside of his physical limits. He blinked the sting of sweat out of his eyes.

If only it was as easy to push his mind to such extremes so he wouldn't have to think.

"Are you trying to kill yourself?" Ben's paramedic partner asked with an amused, almost calculated smile on his face as he watched Ben's struggles from his position as spotter.

"Two more reps," Ben wheezed through his teeth as an alternative to answering the question his friend had not-so-innocently posed. His arms and chest burned with the effort of pushing the bar up twice more, but he was determined to succeed in his efforts, if only because Zach was watching.

Zach helped him return the bar to the rack. Groaning, Ben rolled to a sitting position on the bench.

"I don't know what you're talking about," Ben denied, shaking his head and not quite meeting his friend's gaze. He dabbed at his forehead with the white towel he'd draped around his neck.

"Benching two hundred pounds? That's a bit much even for you, big guy. What if I hadn't been there to spot you and your muscles had seized up on you?"

"But you were there, weren't you?" Ben snapped, scowling at his friend.

Instead of offending him, it only made Zach chuckle all the more.

"Seriously, dude. You've got it bad." Zach's snicker turned into a full-blown laugh. "So tell me—who is the lucky lady?"

"I'm glad I amuse you," Ben retorted. "And I don't know what you're talking about." He really, *really* didn't want to get into this, especially with Zach, whom he considered one of his best friends. The guy wouldn't stop razzing him for a month of Sundays if he learned the truth about what was really going on in Ben's mind.

"Right. So, here's the thing, bro," Zach stated sagely. "The only possible reason for you to be pushing yourself so hard is so you don't have time to think. And if you're trying not to think, it must have something to do with a woman."

Zach nodded shrewdly. "Trust me. I've been there. I know from whence I speak."

Ben snorted. Zach actually did have firsthand knowledge where women were concerned. He'd been the town bad boy from the time he was in school until he'd become a Christian years later. Now he was happily married to his high-school sweetheart, Delia, and was the father of two boys.

Unfortunately for Ben, Zach thought every-one should share in his happiness and find wed-ded bliss themselves. Like marriage was the answer to every problem. Ben scoffed. As far as he was concerned, anything to do with a woman was merely the beginning of all prob-lems.

Vee Bishop being a case in point.

"Who is she? I want a name." Zach smirked and raised a dark eyebrow over his equally dark eyes.

Ben grunted and moved to the inverted sit-up board, hooking his legs over the top beam for stabilization. Then he started performing a furious round of sit-ups, mentally counting as he went.

Twenty. Twenty-one. Twenty-two.

Zach was still hovering, and Ben didn't like the telltale gleam in his friend's eye. Just because *Zach* happened to be enamored of the married state didn't mean Ben had to be.

Fifty-seven. Fifty-eight. Fifty-nine.

"Now you've got me really curious," Zach remarked blithely. "I don't buy your original denial, by the way. You answered too fast, and you're fighting too hard."

Eighty-three. Eighty-four. Eighty-five.

Ben's abdominal muscles were burning, but he didn't let up the frantic pace of his movements.

Ninety-two. Ninety-three. Ninety-four.

"You know I can stand here all day, bud. I've got nothing else to do—unless there's a fire somewhere, and you know as well as I do that's not likely to happen."

One hundred.

Ben swung his legs around and stood, facing down his friend with the biggest scowl he could muster. Could the man just *please* leave it alone? But no, Zach was still grinning at him with an I-won't-quit attitude in his eyes.

"Not one woman. Two," Ben growled under his breath but loud enough for Zach to hear him. He didn't know if he was more exasperated with his situation or with Zach being such an utter nuisance.

"I'm sorry. I don't think I heard you correctly," Zach said, cupping his ear, although it was clear from the look on his face that he'd heard every word perfectly well. "Did you just say you're having issues with *two* women?"

Ben grunted noncommittally.

Zach snorted and shook his head. "Well, no wonder you're doing enough sit-ups to kill a lesser man. Not the best idea, dude, trying to deal with two ladies at the same time. Women are pretty possessive creatures. It doesn't pay to cross one, in my experience."

"Tell me about it," Ben groaned, stepping onto the treadmill and setting the controls for an easy jog. "Believe me, I learned my lesson back when I was going out with Olivia Tate. I made the mistake of taking another girl to dinner—just as friends, mind you—but I never heard the end of it. How did I know that the female population has such an extensive, unspoken list of dos and don'ts we men are supposed to conform to?

"I thought I'd gotten over the worst of my problems when I realized that after two or three dates, a girl would expect me to date her exclusively. Olivia and I had 'the talk' and everything about how we wouldn't date other people. But I hadn't realized that for Olivia, exclusive meant *exclusive*. Apparently I wasn't even supposed to acknowledge female acquaintances without first clearing it with Olivia, her best friends, her mother and probably a whole host of other women. Man, did I ever get into trouble with that one."

"Yeah, I remember," Zach said, choking back another laugh. "Ouch. I think Olivia might still be a little sore about that one."

Ben blew out a breath and grimaced. "Tell me about it. I think we're finally reconciling enough to be friends, but for the longest time she wouldn't even speak to me. She'd burst into tears if I so much as entered a room where she was."

"Her not speaking to you was probably a good thing, if you ask me. Scorned females rank right up there with grizzly bears and poisonous snakes as the scariest things on the planet." Zach brushed his black hair off his forehead with his palm and chuckled. "But you're avoiding the real topic—your problem. *Problems,*" he corrected himself. "Two women." Zach shook his head and snickered again. "Really, Ben."

"There's this woman…"

"This much I already know," Zach said. "Get to the good stuff. Do I know her? What's her name? What does she look like? And then we'll get to Woman Number Two. Same questions, same order. I'm dying of curiosity here."

"There's the rub," Ben admitted, shaking his head and snorting. "I don't know her full name, and I definitely have no idea what she looks like. 'She' Number One, that is. I know a little bit more about the second woman."

"Come again?" Zach said incredulously. "Now, let me get this straight. You have a problem with a girlfriend you've never actually seen and whose name you do not know." Zach whistled in surprise.

Ben punched the control to set the treadmill into a full-out run and wiped his brow with the blue towel draped around his neck.

"I didn't say she was my girlfriend."

"But you obviously have some feelings for her or you wouldn't be bench-pressing two hundred pounds."

"I do care about her. It's not that."

"So what's the problem? I don't get it. Given that you don't know what she looks like, I'm guessing you met on the internet, right? But don't people usually post their pictures on those dating sites?"

"Oh, no. It wasn't a dating site." Ben scoffed and shook his head, causing sweat to drip over his forehead and sting his eyes. "You think I'm that desperate?" He paused. "No, don't answer that."

Zach's dark eyes glittered puckishly and his lips quirked as if he was forcing himself to hold back his ridicule, but he didn't say anything.

"I'm taking an online Spanish class," Ben explained. "I thought it would be a good idea to get a second language under my belt before going off on my mission. Anyway, I got hooked up with her, Veronica Jayne, on a group project."

"And you fell for her." It wasn't a question, but Ben treated it that way.

Ben shrugged noncommittally. "Kind of. Well, I mean, I have to admit I've thought about it. She's a really nice girl. We've been privately emailing each other for weeks now, and we have great conversations together."

"*Conversations?* She's a *nice girl?* Seriously, dude?" Zach barked out a laugh. "You are so clueless."

Ben tensed at the insult, almost causing him to lose his balance on the treadmill. He turned it down to a walk so he could cool down—both his body and his temper.

"And it doesn't bother you *at all* that you don't know her last name and have no idea what she looks like?" Zach made it sound like Ben was crazy for not demanding a picture right away. Would that have made any difference in how his friendship with her had progressed? He hoped he was better than that.

"Of course I've wondered." He stopped the treadmill, stepped off and leaned over to stretch his calves. He averted his gaze from Zach's, staring at his own toes to avoid having to see the amusement in his partner's eyes.

"But you never asked for a photograph?"

"I didn't want to scare her away. Besides, if I did that, she'd want a picture of me, and that *would* scare her away. Same with our last names. I wouldn't want her doing an internet search on me. I know it'll happen eventually, but I'll cross that bridge when I come to it."

Zach tilted his head. "Dude, have you looked in the mirror recently? You're not exactly Quasimodo."

"I have a mental picture of her," Ben responded defensively. "She says she works in a flower shop. She's really feminine. I imagine her wearing floral dresses that go down to her ankles, and I'm positive she has pretty hair and kind eyes."

"And a long, hooked nose. And pointed teeth. And don't forget green skin," Zach added, chortling in amusement at himself. The guy was always clowning around, but Ben wasn't in the mood for a joke.

He stiffened, ready to take offense, but then he started thinking about it, and he had to admit Zach had a point. He shook his head and laughed. It was funny. He was taking everything way too seriously.

"In all honesty, I've been thinking about asking her for a picture of herself for a while now, now that we know each other fairly well. I wouldn't say it's a romantic relationship. Not yet, anyway. I can't deny the thought has occurred to me on more than one occasion that it might turn into one at some point. We've been talking about meeting in person once we've committed to Sacred Heart."

"What's Sacred Heart?"

"A Christian stateside mission. They help people in disasters with food and shelter and such and also try to take care of their spiritual needs. Veronica Jayne and I are both applying to serve there."

Zach whistled. "Cool. I knew you were interested in doing Christian mission work eventually, but I guess I didn't know you were heading that way so soon. So how long would it be until you enlist?"

"Not long now. We both want to finish our Spanish course, and then we'll meet in the summer for orientation at a facility they have in Houston."

"But now you don't want to wait that long to meet her."

"No. I don't. I don't think I can because of something Vee said."

Zach raised his brows. "Vee Bishop?"

"Yeah. You remember how she dressed up for the Easter banquet? Blue dress? High heels?"

Zach laughed. "Apparently I don't remember it as well as you do," he teased. "No, seriously. Everybody in town knows about Vee's presto change-o, frumpy-dumpy into super-gorgeous woman that no man could keep his eyes off of. Even people who weren't there at the banquet have heard about it by now. You know how Jo is about spreading the gossip around—especially something as interesting as that."

"Vee isn't frumpy-dumpy," Ben retorted protectively. "I don't know how she felt, but the whole thing made me uncomfortable. I know she was aware of it. People were treating her differently. Better." Ben knew he sounded defensive in his tone, but he couldn't seem to help it.

"Well, I'll be," Zach said, his eyes narrowing on Ben. "I never would have guessed *that* one."

"Excuse me?"

"You have a thing for Vee Bishop. She's Woman Number Two, isn't she?"

The way Zach said it, he almost sounded like one of the elementary-school bullies Ben had had such problems with growing up. *Ben and Vee, sitting in a tree. K-I-S-S-I-N-G.*

Kissing Vee? Ben swallowed the emotion that rose into his throat, not even wanting to acknowledge it was there. He wasn't ready to go where his thoughts were leading him. He didn't even want to identify whatever feeling it was that was swelling inside his chest.

Hence, working out at the gym until his muscles were screaming, though he would never tell Zach that. Veronica Jayne had only been a part of it.

"I don't have a thing for Vee." His denial sounded false even to his own ears.

"Right."

"Okay," Ben amended. "Maybe I do have a little problem with Vee. Ever since the banquet I can't seem to get her out of my mind. The way she looked when I first saw her across the room in that gorgeous blue dress, so slender and beautiful—I can't even begin to describe it. And her eyes..." He shook his head.

"It sounds to me like *other people* weren't the only ones who were seeing Vee in a different light."

Ben sighed and dropped his gaze to his shoes. He was ashamed of himself. "You're right about that. And that's what bothers me."

"That you have feelings for Vee?" Zach picked up a set of free weights and started working his biceps again.

"No. That I didn't *realize* I might have feelings for Vee until she showed up in that knockout dress." Ben's muscles had had enough torture for one day, so he straddled a bench and leaned back on his arms instead of joining his partner with the free weights. "What kind of a man does that make me?"

"Human," Zach answered immediately. "Maybe you knew you had feelings for Vee and you just didn't want to admit it to yourself."

"Maybe. But it still bothers me that I could be so shallow. I thought I was better than that, which was why I didn't mind that Veronica Jayne and I didn't exchange pictures. God isn't concerned with appearances. He looks at people's hearts."

"That's true," Zach agreed. "But God also made women incredibly attractive to men. It's in our nature for us to notice when an especially pretty woman walks by. I don't think there is anything necessarily wrong with that."

"For me, there is. Going all brainless around beautiful women is one of my stumbling blocks. I got into a lot of trouble when I first got back into town after serving in the National Guard and started dating again. All of a sudden there were dozens of pretty girls who wanted to hang out with me—with *me*—and it went to my head. I made a lot of bad decisions and stupid mistakes. Mistakes that ended up hurting people I cared about. I don't want that to happen again, and I'm terrified it might. I've got to reel it in. Do you understand what I mean?"

"Which is why you're so flipped out about this other girl, Veronica Jayne, right?"

"Exactly. I don't want to mess up our friendship because I can't handle it when I find out what she really looks like. What if I don't find her attractive? I know—that makes me super shallow, right?"

"And Vee? She's back to her old hair-in-a-bun, super-tough-attitude self now, you know."

Ben sighed internally. It didn't matter to him what Vee wore. It didn't even matter that she'd always disliked him. He had feelings for her either way. Which was entirely irrelevant, not only to this conversation, but to his life.

"It doesn't matter how I feel about Vee. She can't even stand to be in the same room with me. It seems like she's just barely tolerating my presence when I'm around her, though I think it's been a little bit better lately."

"You've told her how you feel?"

"Of course not. But I can tell you without a doubt that she has some kind of problem with me. I only wish I knew what it was."

Zach burst out laughing, and it took him a moment to contain himself enough to speak. He was holding his belly, snorting and huffing.

Ben rolled his eyes.

"Dude, you really are clueless."

"You think?" In Ben's opinion, *clueless* didn't even begin to cover it.

"Seriously. You really don't know why she doesn't like you very much?"

Ben shook his head and made a bowing motion with his hands. "Enlighten me, oh wise one."

"You just told me what your problem is." Zach flashed a knowing grin.

"And that would be?" Ben was a little annoyed at the way his friend was dragging this out, but at least it seemed like he had an answer to Ben's problem. Zach did know women. After all, he was married to one.

"Vee's best friend is Olivia Tate," Zach explained, drawing out the words as if Ben would be slow to comprehend.

Which he definitely was.

"Olivia," Zach repeated. "Vee's best friend. Your ex-girlfriend. Just think about it."

Chapter Nine

Vee stared at the blank computer screen and sipped absently at her caramel latte. She was in her usual place in the back corner of Cup o' Jo's Café, but this was anything but a usual day.

She had to break things off with BJ, and she didn't know how she was going to do that.

No, that wasn't quite right. It wasn't as if she and BJ were actually an item, so it wasn't like they were breaking up or anything. But they were both well aware that the potential to become more than just friends had been there since the first day they'd met. They'd even talked about it, making the decision to wait until they met in person at the Sacred Heart Mission to pursue anything further, anything that might be construed as romantic.

But she had to be honest and admit, at least to herself, that even after they'd come to their agreement, she'd harbored these now preposterous-sounding private fantasies about the moment when she and BJ would finally meet in person for the first time...

She's at the first orientation meeting for the Sacred Heart Mission. Seated at the far end of the room, she's scanning through the packet of informational materials she'd been given, excited to finally be pursuing her ambitions. She's finally here, making her dreams a reality. Her heart is pumping, and her mind is swirling in dizzy circles with all the adrenaline pumping through her.

Suddenly it's as if the atmosphere itself grows warmer. More humid. Harder to breathe. She knows instinctively that BJ has entered the room.

She glances toward the door, knowing this moment is going to change her life—change both of their lives. Her eyes meet BJ's, and the world is turned on its axis.

He is the most handsome man she's ever laid eyes on, just as she knew in her heart that he'd be, and better than she could even have imagined.

Reality alters when he smiles, and she knows for certain that they'll be together forever.

She has found true love.

Ridiculous. Pure, utter poppycock.

She had to let it go and get on with her life. Her *real* life.

And that meant being brutally honest with both herself and with BJ. She respected him enough to want to clarify her new perspective directly and without any delay.

She'd been living in this fantasy world of Prince-Charming-rides-in-to-save-the-day for long enough. She hadn't realized the truth about her relationship with BJ until the day Ben had come with her to visit her father, when reality had struck her like a slap to the face. She was using BJ to avoid real life because she couldn't handle the grief she felt after her mother's death.

She was hiding in cyberspace.

And it was time to come back to earth.

She didn't know if it would be a wise idea to remain friends with BJ at all, as much as she liked him as a person. She wasn't sure she could completely annihilate the fantasy, and if she couldn't, she could never embrace the reality.

She supposed she could wait until they met in person at the mission to make any final decisions on the matter. If, indeed, they ended up at the same mission at all. Vee was having her doubts about that, too. Maybe it would be better for both of them if she applied to a different agency and they made a clean break. Perhaps they should simply finish their Spanish project and call it all good between them.

The internet provided a false sense of intimacy. And she was no longer kidding herself—it *was* false. A woman could present herself any way she wanted to be—and Vee had done just that. Yes, in some ways she had been more open with BJ than with anyone else—she hadn't been lying when she'd said that he knew her better than anyone else. She'd felt comfortable showing him parts of her personality that no one else knew about. But she hadn't shown him everything. Veronica Jayne was who she was, but there were distinct differences in how she'd presented herself online and the way the people in Serendipity saw her.

No doubt BJ had done the same. Maybe there were other sides to him beyond the strong, soft-spoken man Vee imagined him to be.

There was absolutely no way to know if they'd even get along in person, much less be romantically inclined toward one another. They'd never even exchanged pictures, though they'd been emailing each other personally for at least a couple of months.

Who did that?

Naturally, she'd pictured BJ to be a handsome man with bold features and strong arms, but for all she knew the guy had a hump on his back.

Even worse, lately when she imagined what BJ looked like, the image of Ben Atwood persistently entered her mind—probably because he was, in fact, the best-looking man she knew. Objectively speaking, that is.

And how messed up was that?

Must. Face. Reality.

"Okay," said a light, lilting voice from the other side of her computer screen. Olivia, of course, with the worst timing ever. "I have *got* to know what it is you were thinking about just now."

Ben.

Vee was thinking about Ben. She certainly couldn't say that out loud—especially to Olivia.

"If you must know, I've been keeping a secret from you," Vee said on a sigh. That ought to pique Olivia's interest enough to keep her from suspecting Vee's mind was anywhere close to dwelling on her ex-boyfriend.

It did. "Oooh! Secrets. I love to hear about secrets. Spill it, girlfriend." She set her plate on the table and slid into the chair across from Vee.

Olivia was the exact opposite of Vee—her tall, graceful body was highlighted with short, thick, pixie-cut red hair she'd gotten from her mother's Scottish roots and emerald-green eyes that had at one time or another enthralled practically every single man in the town. Not only that, but Olivia was as bubbly and outgoing as Vee was reserved and antisocial. Yet somehow despite the odds they'd become fast friends in elementary school and had remained that way throughout their adulthood.

"I'm warning you—this one's a doozy."

"Better and better," Olivia murmured, leaning closer so she could share the moment.

"There's this man…"

Olivia squealed loud enough for many of the patrons sharing a meal at Cup o' Jo to turn and glance in their direction, curiosity written on their faces.

"Olivia," Vee begged, "will you please be quiet about this? I'd rather not have the whole world aware that I have a problem."

"Okay, okay," Olivia agreed, scooting around to Vee's side of the table, pulling her cheeseburger and French-fry-laden plate along with her. "Now, spill the beans. Who is this man, and why have I not heard about him?" She peered at the empty computer monitor as if she'd find the answer there.

"His name is BJ." Vee nodded toward the computer screen. "I met him in my online Spanish class. We're doing a project together on the advantages of knowing the Spanish language when we work in stateside Christian missions."

"Sounds intriguing," Olivia said, popping a

French fry into her mouth. "The man, not the topic," she clarified with a laugh. "Although that's interesting, too. So he's going to be doing this stateside mission thing with you? And *habla español* a little bit between you?" She waggled her eyebrows.

Vee nudged Olivia with her elbow. "Cut it out. Knowing how to speak a little Spanish will be very important in the line of work I'm planning to do."

"Of course," Olivia agreed. "You know I'm just joshing with you."

Vee chuckled and nodded. "Yeah. I know. I'm easy bait. And I have to admit that the whole man thing *is* interesting. Or should I say *complicated*."

"Hey, Vee." She hadn't seen Ben enter the café, much less realized that he'd approached her table—with Olivia sitting right there, to boot. "How are you doing tonight? And you, Olivia?" he continued, though his gaze stayed on Vee.

His bronze-green gaze held hers, and his toothy smile made her stomach do a somersault. Transparently gorgeous any way she looked at him. And for some reason he was only looking at *her*.

She shouldn't be looking at him at all, especially not with her best friend present. She dropped her gaze to the tabletop and searched for something to say, something that wouldn't make her sound like an idiot. She couldn't seem to be able to form words. The thoughts were in her head, but nothing came out of her mouth. She was afraid if she tried to speak it would come out garbled. Then she really *would* sound like an idiot.

Tension mounted as each excruciating second ticked by. Sweat trickled down the nape of Vee's neck. She didn't know how long it was until Olivia noisily cleared her throat, but it felt like an eternity, and a painful one at that.

"Yes, that's right. I'm here, too, though I can clearly see why you didn't notice me," Olivia said with a teasing laugh that bordered on flirtatious.

Vee stared at her friend in shock. She had expected Olivia to be mad. She would have been if she was in the same situation.

At least Ben had the grace to look chagrined, his lips twisting as he considered what to say.

Olivia laughed again, beaming a hundred-watt smile at Ben, who shifted uncomfortably.

"I think my food's ready," he said awkwardly, brushing his hand back through the dark curl falling down over his forehead. "I guess I'll see you ladies later. Have a good might. Meal. Night," he stammered, then shook his head, turned on his heels and practically ran for his table.

Vee mused silently as she watched Ben stride across the room and slide into a booth with his back toward her. He must have sensed her gaze upon him because he turned and winked at her.

Vee slid an inch lower in her booth, as if somehow that would make her inconspicuous, because at the moment she felt as if she was wearing an enormous exclamation point on her head.

"Well," commented Olivia in a drawn-out syllable. It wasn't a question. Vee shivered.

"Well?" Vee repeated without acknowledging that she had any indication of where Olivia's train of thought had gone. "Do you want to tell me what just happened here between you and Ben, or do you want me to guess? Because if I guess, I can guarantee it's going to be more interesting than anything you can make up on the spur of the moment. I thought you guys weren't talking to one another. *He broke my heart and I'll never fall in love again,* and all that."

"I'm over it." Olivia shrugged. "Actually, I'm more interested in what happened between *you* and Ben."

Vee ignored her. This was not about her. "You're actually speaking to him again?"

"Sure. This isn't junior high anymore. I don't like drama."

Vee had to contain her urge to snort. Olivia Tate was one of the biggest drama queens she knew. But she appeared to be serious about this, so Vee let her continue.

"We live in the same small town. It's inevitable that we'll run into each other from time to time, especially because we both go to the same church."

"That's very mature of you," Vee stated blandly.

Olivia burst into shrill laughter that made a few heads turn. "Really, Vee. You kill me, sometimes."

"Maybe you can get over it, but I can't. I have a long memory. He hurt my best friend, and that's all there is to say about it."

"That's always been a problem for you," said Olivia, suddenly serious. "You always stick up for the underdog." She reached out and gave Vee's hand a squeeze. "My little pit bull. I know you love me, but I'm okay now. When I look back on what happened now, I see that it wasn't all his fault. I need to take some of the blame, too."

Vee's jaw dropped. "He cheated on you! He was going out with another woman after the two of you had decided to date exclusively. How could that be your fault?"

"He definitely took another woman out, but I'm not sure they were actually dating."

"What?"

Olivia shrugged. "He told me at the time that she was just a friend. I didn't believe him then, but now I think he might have been telling the truth."

"Wh-what changed your mind?" Vee couldn't help asking.

"He has. Or rather, his ex-girlfriends have. See, back then I was sure he was playing me false, not just because he had dinner with his so-called 'friend,' but because when I confronted him about it he didn't even try to change my mind. I told him to leave, and he left. I told him never to call me again...and he didn't. I thought that meant he didn't care about me, that our relationship hadn't mattered to him at all."

"What does that have to do with his ex-girlfriends?"

Olivia grinned. "Well, over the years, I've found myself comparing notes with a lot of girls our Mr. Atwood has dated, and I've reached some new conclusions." She paused, clearly waiting for a signal from Vee.

"Fine," Vee said, rolling her eyes at her overly dramatic friend. "I'll ask—what new conclusions?"

"I think he's just really clueless about women."

"But how is that possible? He's dated so many!"

"Yeah," Olivia agreed. "And the reason he's dated so many is because he finds some ridiculous way to mess his relationships up. One girl told me she broke up with him because he'd never call her back after she called him—but she admitted that when she left messages, she'd usually say something like 'Nothing's wrong, I was just calling to hear your voice. You don't have to call me back.' So he didn't.

"Another girl made him go with her when she went shopping. And when she asked him if a dress made her look fat..."

"He said it did," Vee filled in, seeing where this was going.

Olivia giggled. "Let's just say he didn't lie to her. So after our big fight, when I told him to get out and never call me again..."

"He left. And never called you again."

"Bingo. Yes, he hurt me. Yes, he should have known better. But it wasn't all his fault. You can let it rest. I promise my feelings won't be hurt if you do."

"Do what?" asked Vee, confused.

Olivia winked. "You know."

"Uh-uh. I don't. And I'm not sure I want to."

Olivia merely shrugged and flashed a knowing grin. "You don't want to talk about it. Okay. So tell me more about this cyber-hunk of yours."

"Where to start? His writing flows like music. Like a symphony of words. Mushy as all get-out and sweet as a daisy in the springtime. I'm afraid I got a little too caught up in that."

"What girl wouldn't?"

"In some ways I feel like I know BJ very well, but in other ways I really don't know anything about him. I've never even seen what he looks like."

"You have got to be kidding me. You're getting all twitterpated over a man when you've never even seen his face? Girl, you *are* a mess."

"Tell me about it," Vee agreed with a miserable groan. "But I'm not *twitterpated,* as you put it. Actually, I'm trying to figure out a way to back out gracefully without hurting his feelings."

"But why? Maybe you'll meet him face-to-face and fall instantly and madly in love." She sighed dramatically. So much for not being a drama queen.

Vee met her friend's gaze and lifted her eyebrows. "Can you not see why I have a problem, here? This whole relationship is a sham."

Olivia's shoulders slumped. "I suppose. When you put it that way. So what are you going to tell him?"

"I have no idea. That would be the reason behind the expression you saw on my face when you walked up." Vee wiggled the computer mouse to light up the screen.

She pulled up her email. There was a note from BJ.

Dear Veronica Jayne,
We've been corresponding for months now, and I feel like I know you pretty well. I hope you feel the same about me. We aren't strangers anymore, are we?

What do you think about exchanging pictures? I'd like to see what my flower girl really looks like.
Sincerely,
BJ

"Veronica Jayne? *Flower girl?*" Olivia was definitely getting her jollies at Vee's expense. She was enjoying this *way* too much.

"Veronica Jayne is my online handle. It also happens to be my given name, thank you very much. It says so right on my birth certificate. He calls me his flower girl because that's what I told him I do for a living—I work with flowers. Which is also true."

"Kinda. Not firefighting?"

"Me in my firefighter's garb. Now *there's* an attractive image. No, thank you."

"Hey! I'm here to tell you that you rock that uniform. There's absolutely nothing wrong with you being a female firefighter."

"No, I know that. I was going for something a little different, you know? Everyone here in Serendipity sees the no-nonsense firefighter who's just one of the guys, which is not particularly good for my love life. I guess I wanted to present a different side of myself, something a little more soft and feminine."

"Oh, I get it," Olivia responded. "You think that since you've only shown him the 'girlie' parts of you that he won't like the rest. Is that why you want out?"

"That's part of it, I suppose. But it goes the other way, too. He might not like the parts of me I haven't shown him—and I might not like the parts of him he hasn't put on display. Who knows what he's really like in person?"

"I think you should wait and find out. See how things go when you guys meet face-to-face."

"No, I need to do this now."

"Before you've seen what he looks like, even?"

Before she lost her nerve, more like.

"He's offering to send you a picture of himself. Are you seriously trying to tell me you aren't the least bit curious if he's handsome or not?"

"Of course I am."

"Then let him send you a photograph. He was the one who offered, right? You get to see what he looks like, and then you can tell him you just want to be friends or whatever. What's the harm in that?"

"I don't know. I get all jittery when I think about it. What if he's nothing like the man I pictured in my head?"

"So what if he isn't? You said yourself it didn't matter what he looked like."

"But what if he *is*, Olivia? What if he's the most attractive man I've ever seen? What am I going to do then?"

Olivia glanced across the room at Ben and flicked her chin in his direction. "I highly doubt that your BJ guy is going to be the best-looking guy you've ever laid eyes on. I saw the way your gaze lit up when Ben stopped by our table."

"No you did not," Vee responded adamantly. She wanted to crawl underneath the table and hide there. Maybe dig a hole to China and forget learning Spanish. Not only was she struggling with an attraction to a man who no doubt looked at her as nothing more than an annoying coworker at best, but her very best friend Olivia, ex-girlfriend of said attractive man, was picking up on it.

This was bad. Really bad.

"Ben looked at you the same way," Olivia stated as matter-of-factly as if she were reciting the weather forecast. "I wouldn't mind, you know—if you and Ben got together. You'd make an adorable couple."

Vee was embarrassed—humiliated—that her emotions were running so close to the surface. This wasn't like her, and it made her more uncomfortable than she could say.

"And now that he's had some time to grow up a little bit, he's probably less clueless about women. He's certainly gotten smarter about dating every woman in town," Olivia continued. Same song, different verse. "Ben isn't the same fresh boy that he was when he came back to town from the military. He's matured. And you've got to admit he *is* pretty sweet-looking. You two would look so cute together. I really wouldn't mind."

Vee shook her head furiously. "*I'd* mind. Can we please not talk about this anymore?"

"Okay," agreed Olivia easily. "Then let's get back to your cyber-guy. Picture or no picture?"

Vee stared at BJ's email for a moment before pressing reply. She typed in a single word in response.

Okay.

Chapter Ten

Okay.

Ben stared at the one-word email. Veronica Jayne wanted to exchange pictures with him. His heart raced so hard that it roared in his ears.

What did his flower girl really look like? Was she blonde? Brunette? Tall? Short?

More to the point, would it matter? It was time for him to discover if he had any depth of character whatsoever or, as he feared, if he was just as shallow as the next guy, not able to look past a pretty face into something more substantial and meaningful.

Veronica Jayne hadn't attached a photograph of herself, so he assumed she wanted him to go first. He used his mouse to click the folder containing his digital pictures and scrolled through them, searching for a photo of himself that put him at best advantage and that he imagined Veronica Jayne might like.

There was one of him and Zach panning goofy for the camera, their arms slung over each other's shoulders, but he quickly nixed that one. He didn't want to confuse Veronica Jayne by sending her a picture of two guys, he reflected with a startled chuckle. What if she thought Zach was the better-looking of the two of them?

Ben wasn't willing to take *that* chance. Zach Bowden had turned more than a few women's heads in the years before he'd married and settled down. What kind of comparison was there between the two men? Ben didn't even want to know.

He finally settled on a picture his mother had snapped of him on a Sunday afternoon over the dinner table. It was a close-up of his face, and he was smiling his natural smile. It would have to do.

He hit Reply and attached the photograph to the email, then poised his fingers over the keys to write her a short note.

Dear Veronica Jayne,
Well, here it is. Or rather, here I am. I have to admit I'm a little nervous about what you'll think of me. Don't judge too harshly. I'm look-

ing forward to receiving a photograph of you so I can finally put a face to your lovely name. Veronica Jayne. My flower girl.
BJ

"Hey, Uncle Ben," Felix called as Ben's two nephews scampered into the room. "What are you doing? Mom said you're supposed to take us to the church carnival."

Ben closed his laptop with a snap and laughed as he rounded up his nephews and tickled their ribs. "I was just finishing up some work here. You guys are anxious to go to the carnival, huh?"

"Yeah, yeah," the boys answered in unison.

"Impatient little rugrats." He ruffled their hair. "Are you ready to throw rings at pop bottles and win the cakewalk?"

"What's a cakewalk?" Nigel asked, screwing his face into an adorably bemused expression, his dark brows lowered over expressive eyes. "Do we really get to walk on cakes?"

Ben barked out a laugh. "No, little man. You don't walk *on* cakes. You win one if you're the last person standing. Or sitting, technically. In a chair." The two boys shared confused looks and he shook his head. "It's hard to explain. You'll just have to learn to play it when you get there."

Ben bundled the boys in their jackets and they headed out.

It was only a couple of blocks to the church from his parents' house, so he and the boys walked, enjoying the temperate spring air. Felix and Nigel were both squirrelly from being cooped up in the house all day, and Ben thought it would be good for them to run off some of that energy before entering the carnival, which would be a crush of people in a relatively small area.

He was in excellent physical shape, but it was all he could do to keep up with the little guys, and he gained a new appreciation for mothers who had to herd their kids around day in and day out.

Located on the northeast corner of town on Main Street, the parking lot of the little white chapel was already full to overflowing with vehicles. Festive music streamed from the open doors of the fellowship hall, and he could already hear the joyous sound of children's laughter, which made him smile. Nigel and Felix picked up their pace, dashing into the building ahead of Ben.

"Come one, come all," greeted Jo exuberantly as Ben entered through the double doors. "Come eager to spend your money for a good cause—new choir robes for our trusty sanctuary choir! Hey there, Ben. Are you and the boys ready to win some prizes?"

Jo sounded like an old-time carnival barker, adding to the already festive ambiance. Ben suspected that in Jo's mind, at least, the *good cause* in question might have been more to do with the kiddos having fun than having anything to do with the state of the choir's worn-out robes.

"Did you see my nephews pass by?" he asked.

Jo waved a hand over her shoulder. "They just went by here, somewhere about the speed of light. Good luck finding them in that throng of people."

It *was* crowded. And noisy. But Ben wasn't worried for his nephews. Townspeople looked after their own, and a couple of extra boys running around was no cause for concern.

Ben had helped set up the booths for the carnival the evening before so he knew what to expect. The fellowship hall had been divided into a series of separate booths draped with colorful cloths and signs and flashing lights—mostly red and green, donations from town folks' Christmas collections.

A rubbery bounce house and a hay maze had been set up in the field behind the church, with an oil-drum train circling the whole thing. Chief Jenkins engineered the train, and he whistled and tooted at frequent intervals just to keep things lively, as if there wasn't already enough clamor in the neighborhood.

"What do you guys want to do first?" he asked as he caught up to his nephews, who were leaning over a booth to watch Riley Bowden, Zach's eldest son, toss beanbags at a cardboard rendering of Noah's Ark. There were several animals painted on the Ark, their mouths cut open for the kids to toss beanbags through. Eleven-year-old Riley was a good shot and two of his three beanbags sailed through the holes into the lion's and hippo's mouths.

Phoebe Hawkins, who was manning the beanbag toss, cheered for Riley as he picked out his prize—a straw cowboy hat, which he planted on his head with pride. Ben congratulated the boy on his good aim.

Ben fished a wad of dollar bills from the front pocket of his jeans, intending to spend every one of them. Each year the carnival had a different charitable goal in mind. After they'd collected enough money to buy the choir some decent robes, whatever was left over would go to the church's food bank. Ben couldn't think of a better way to contribute to the ministry of the church than to fork over a little cash to watch his nephews have a good time.

"Uncle Ben, Uncle Ben," Nigel exclaimed,

grabbing his hand and pulling him toward the booth across the way from the Noah's Ark Beanbag Toss. "Look! Goldfish!"

Sure enough, there were the goldfish, swimming around in gallon-sized plastic bags full of water that were stacked enticingly along the back counter.

"Anyone want to win a goldfish?" Vee's wry chuckle snapped Ben from his reverie. He looked up to find her grinning craftily at him.

He narrowed his gaze on her. "You planned this, didn't you?"

Vee shook her head and scoffed, but her smile remained. "Right. I ran out and bought three dozen goldfish because I knew it would entice your nephews and annoy you."

"I wouldn't put it past you," he objected, but he smiled back at her nonetheless. "How do you win one of these fellows, anyway?"

Vee pointed to a plastic pool half-filled with water in which a couple dozen identical yellow rubber ducks floated. "Pick a winner. Small, medium or large prizes, depending on what's written on the bottom of the ducky you select. You boys want to try?" she asked, addressing Felix and Nigel.

In hindsight, Ben realized he should have been more cognizant of what was going on in each of the booths so he could avoid instant goldfish ownership, but it was too late now, with both of his nephews clamoring to have a go at the duckies. It wasn't like he could say no to them. It would ruin their day. Besides, Ben remembered being thrilled to win a goldfish when he was a kid. He wouldn't deny his nephews the same happy memory.

"That will be two bucks," Vee reminded him, holding out her hand palm up.

Ben peeled two fresh dollar bills from his wad of cash and passed them off to Vee. "I want you to know I am doing this under duress."

"No you're not," she replied without hesitating. "You're doing this because you are a good uncle and you want to give your nephews a day they'll remember."

"If they win goldfish, this is going to be a day *I'll* remember," he groused. "Thanks to you."

"Oh, hush, you, and let the poor boys have their fun." She turned to Felix and Nigel. "Okay, you guys, it's time to play. You each get to pick up only one duck, so choose carefully, all right? Ready? Set? Go!"

Felix plucked his duck out of the water within seconds. Nigel was not quite so hasty with his choice, taking his time to select the perfect duck. Several times he started for one and then changed his mind and pulled his hand back."

"You've got to pick one, Nigel," Ben urged.

Nigel finally made his choice. The boys turned their ducks over at the same time.

"Large," announced Vee in a voice Ben was certain was lined with laughter. "And large. Congratulations, boys, you've each won yourselves a goldfish."

Felix and Nigel high-fived each other.

Vee laughed, and Ben wondered if she was laughing with him or at him.

He groaned, but it was more of an exasperated, dramatic gesture than a meaningful one.

"You've got this rigged, don't you? I'll bet every one of these ducks has an *L* on it."

"Well, that would be very kind of me if that were true, don't you think?" She plucked a random duck from the pool and turned it over, waving it under his nose so he'd be sure to see the *S* clearly marked on the bottom. "But in this case, it's not true. I think you were meant to own goldfish, Ben Atwood."

If it were anyone but Vee, he would have thought she was flirting with him. But it *was* Vee—and Vee didn't flirt. With anyone.

Especially not with him.

So why did his gut tighten in response to her repartee, and why was his breath raspy in his throat? He needed to tread softly here.

"Maybe I'll just feed the fish to Tinker," he remarked mildly.

He'd clearly caught her off-guard with the statement. He hadn't meant it, of course, but it was fun teasing her. "You wouldn't," she said, her voice hitched with hesitation and distress in her gaze.

He flashed her a toothy grin, stepping back and slapping a hand over his heart. "No, of course not. I'm wounded here. Seriously, Vee, do you think I'm capable of fish-ocide?"

"I think you're capable of a lot of things," she said under her breath, shaking her head.

What was that supposed to mean? The woman spoke in riddles. And unfortunately for him, he didn't speak *woman.*

He would have demanded an explanation in plain, understandable English except that several other children were congregating around her booth and she'd turned her attention to them.

That, and the fact that Jo Spencer was yanking at his sleeve.

"It's nearly your turn, dear," she said, loud enough to be heard over the din of the crowd. "Don't you worry a bit about Felix and Nigel. I'll watch them for you. And the goldfish. We can leave them with Vee for later."

"My turn for what?" asked Ben, confused. He'd willingly offered to help set up and take down the booths for the carnival, but other than that he didn't remember signing up for any other duties.

Jo chuckled in delight. "Didn't anyone tell you? No, of course not. Why would they? It was supposed to be a secret."

It sounded to Ben like she was having a running conversation with herself, but he kept an ear out for any vital information she might pass on. "More than one handsome man has been surprised today. Felix, Nigel, come along with your uncle and me. Vee, can you put the boys' names on their goldfish so they can pick them up later?"

"Of course," Vee agreed readily.

"This does not sound good," he remarked as he let Jo lead him down to the end of one row of booths and up another.

"Don't be a spoilsport," Jo scolded. "Now, it's just right outside here."

Ben tensed automatically. Presumably he wasn't going to like whatever *it* was that they were heading toward. Why else would the ladies' church committee, the ones who'd spent so many months planning the carnival, be so hush-hush about it?

"We all wanted this to be a surprise," Jo explained, answering his question as if she'd read his thoughts. "It's going to be the highlight of the day for everyone."

Jo pointed to a spot just beyond the bounce house where—oh, no, it couldn't be.

Oh, yes, it was.

An old-fashioned dunk tank.

Currently, Zach was dangling his legs over the edge of a board hanging well over the tank. He was catcalling everyone within hearing distance, provoking them to take a swing at him. Or a throw, rather. The board was rigged to a twelve-inch-round bull's-eye.

Charlie, one of the younger firefighters, was taking a turn trying to dunk Zach. Three balls later and Zach was still as dry as a bone as he crawled off the board with a triumphant grin on his face.

"See, now?" Jo told Ben. "You probably won't even get wet. And remember, it's—"

"For a good cause," Ben finished for her. "Yeah, I know. I guess it looks okay. The target is obviously hard to hit."

"Believe you me, the mechanism doesn't spring very easily. My three balls didn't make a dent in it. I had to go and press it with my own two hands to dunk Chance into the tank, cowboy hat and all. You should have heard him bellow."

Ben raised a brow.

Jo shrugged nonchalantly. "We had to try it out to make sure it worked, right?"

"So it's hard to spring the latch?" Ben asked again, not at all sure that Jo was being straight with him.

"It's very difficult, yes. In any case, a little water can't hurt a big, strong, hunky guy like you, can it?"

Probably not, but Ben didn't like the idea of getting soaked just the same. He wasn't even wearing swimming trunks. He wondered who'd put his name on the list and conveniently forgot to tell him about it.

"Your turn, buddy," Zach announced, giving him a friendly punch in the shoulder. "We boys have got to do our civic duty, now, don't we?"

"As long as I don't get wet," Ben replied as he tugged off one of his worn black cowboy boots and then the other. He found a tree a little bit out of the way and put his boots and hat aside. If he ended up getting dunked, he wouldn't be as caught off-guard as Chance had evidently been.

Feeling petulant, he climbed up on the board. He was going to do this for the sake of the church, but he didn't have to be cheerful about his *service* the way his partner was.

He didn't announce himself or hoot and holler the way Zach had done. Rather, he sat silently, staring at the crowd. It wasn't long before there was quite a long line, mostly composed of young women, who wanted to take their turns trying to dunk him. Fortunately, no one was a very good shot, and Ben was beginning to think he was going to come away from the experience dry and unscathed.

"Oh, I'm so doing this." Ben recognized Vee's voice at once.

Terrific. He had a sinking feeling *she* wouldn't miss.

Apparently those around her felt the same way, for a cheer rose up from the crowd as she picked up the first of the three baseballs she'd purchased. She took aim and pitched.

The first one went high and wide. The second was off to the left, barely missing the target and causing a collective groan from the audience.

Ben released the breath he'd been holding. Vee wasn't any better a throw than any of the other women before her. He was as good as safe.

But then her determined gaze met his, and Ben knew beyond the shadow of a doubt that he was going to be unceremoniously dropped into the tank full of water.

"Wait a minute," he called. He was probably only delaying the inevitable, but he wasn't going into that water without getting some kind of satisfaction out of it.

"What does she win if she dunks me?" he asked.

A goldfish, maybe?

Ha! That would be justice in the extreme.

"How about a date?" Jo suggested with a chuckle that suggested that this was a calculated proposal.

The folks crowded around the dunking booth put up a crazed cheer.

Whoa.

Ben hadn't seen *that* one coming.

In a panicked haze, he surveyed the gathering, desperately trying to think his way out of the hole he'd dug himself into, but his brain wasn't keeping up with the pounding of his pulse in his head. There was nothing he could think of, no one who could help him, who could save him from his own foolish big mouth. Everyone so clearly approved of Jo's idea that it would have been beyond disrespectful to act as if he were anything but pleased by the idea. Actually, he thought the suggestion had merit, but he doubted Vee would feel the same way about it.

She hadn't seen that fly ball coming, either, for she had the same distressed expression as when he'd suggested that he was going to feed his goldfish to the cat. Her almond-brown eyes were as huge as a doe's in a hunter's light. Her cheeks were scorching red, which was unusual given her dark complexion.

"No, that's all right. No dates, please." Vee

held her hands up as if she were being robbed and backed away from the counter. "I don't need a prize, and I really don't think a date would be a good idea."

Wow. Now *that* stung.

It was the equivalent of his asking her out and her turning him down right in front of the entire community; and although it hadn't been Ben's idea in the first place—exactly—he didn't care to be humiliated in front of his friends and neighbors. Pride burned in his chest.

How could she?

He didn't realize Vee still held the third and final baseball until, a good ten feet or so from the booth, she suddenly spun around on her heels and fired the ball at the target.

Ben heard a metallic *thwump,* and the next moment he was underwater.

Freezing cold water.

By the time he splashed around and finally got his bearings to surface again, Vee was gone.

Vee stayed around long enough to see the satisfaction of her baseball hitting the mark and Ben disappearing underwater, but then she quickly hurried off before someone in the crowd could suggest she collect her *prize.*

What was Jo thinking? She knew the history between Ben and Olivia. Surely she had to know that Vee—

Her feet suddenly refused to move of their own accord. She felt like someone had slapped her in the face.

She knew exactly how that statement ended, and it wasn't good.

Surely Jo had to know that *Vee hadn't forgiven Ben.*

Heat burned her face and she forged ahead, picking up her pace and leaving the church grounds far behind her. She headed down Main Street, making a right toward the park.

She ought to be ashamed of herself. She *was* ashamed. Just the other day Olivia had made it clear that she was willing to let go of her past with Ben, even though she was the one who had been directly hurt.

Who was Vee to hold a grudge when she wasn't even the wronged party? And what about the wrongs she'd done, herself?

Ben had certainly reached out to her on more than one occasion, extending the hand of friendship, which she had brushed aside time and time again. And now she'd humiliated him in front of the whole town.

Not good.

She owed him an apology. A big one.

"Vee, wait!"

Vee froze, her whole body tensing when she heard Ben's voice.

Why had he followed her? To chew her out as she knew she deserved? Yes, she needed to apologize to him, but at this very moment she *so* wasn't ready for this. She hadn't even had time to pray about it, much less consider her words.

"Wait up just a second," Ben called again. He jogged to her side. He'd clearly been running. His breath was coming in low, ragged gasps. He was soaking wet, from his slicked-back black hair to the bottom of his blue jeans.

And he was barefoot.

"You don't have any shoes on," she pointed out, realizing only afterward that she was stating the obvious. Not only that, but it sounded like she was scolding.

He scowled down at her.

"*What* is your problem?" he demanded. "What did I ever do to you?"

She cocked her head. It had never been about what Ben had done to *her*. But clearly he didn't realize that. Olivia was right—he truly was clueless about women. For some reason that made it a lot easier to let go of her anger. He wasn't the callous playboy she'd taken him for. He was just a sweet, naive guy who sometimes did the wrong thing, even if it wasn't on purpose. "You really don't know, do you?"

He shook his head fiercely, confusion gleaming from his eyes. "Obviously not."

"Well, then, I've wasted an awful lot of effort and energy giving you the cold shoulder, and it appears it was all for nothing."

"What?" He moved back a step as if she'd pushed him. He ran his fingers through his wet curls.

"Oh, nothing. I just realized I've been carrying a heavy burden God never meant for me to carry."

His brow lowered. He actually looked concerned for her, though why he should care after the way she'd treated him was beyond her. She'd not only dunked him into a tank of cold water, she'd been the one to put his name in the hat in the first place—a fact that he was probably unaware of. She was the reason he'd been picked for the dunk tank at all.

What had she been thinking?

"Is there anything I can do to help?" His voice was so rich with sincerity and disquiet that it yanked at her heartstrings. If he was any sweeter, he'd have to change his name to *Chocolate*.

"Why are you being nice to me?"

Of course the question came out sounding

defensive. When had she become so cynical? She tried again. "I don't understand you. You should detest me for the way I've treated you."

His gaze widened, and his eyes shimmered with an emotion she did not immediately recognize.

"Vee," he said from deep in his throat. "Do you really not know, honey?"

He reached out tentatively and stroked her cheek with the pad of his thumb, then ran his fingers across her jaw.

She knew she should turn away, but no man had ever looked at her the way Ben was looking at her now. No man had ever touched her with the combination of strength and gentleness he was showing her. No man's fingers had ever quivered as they slid across her cheek, showing vulnerability within that strength.

His other hand joined the first, tenderly framing her face, tipping her chin up with his thumbs.

"Vee?" he said again, but this time it was a question.

She wasn't certain just what she said in that moment. She was pretty sure it wasn't a real word. Probably more like a strangled sigh.

She pressed her palms to his chest. His breath was warm against her cheek and he continued to hold her gaze, but he didn't move a muscle.

Was he waiting for her to push him away?

She didn't. Instead, she tangled her fingers in the wet cotton of his shirt and pulled him toward her, standing on tiptoe until his mouth met hers.

Warmth flooded her senses. Her heartbeat pounded in her ears. The world spun around her and there was nothing but Ben.

Only Ben.

His kiss was tender. Searching. Wonderful.

And it scared her to death.

Vee broke away with a cry of dismay and darted off in the other direction as fast as her shaky legs could carry her.

This time Ben didn't follow her.

Chapter Eleven

Ben wasn't the kind of man to kiss and tell, but he was in a world of trouble, and he didn't know where to turn for help. He was so confused he couldn't even bring himself to return to the church to pick up his nephews. Instead, he'd called Jo Spencer and asked her to bring them—and his hat and his boots—by the house.

Even now, after a restless night's sleep, his head was still swimming.

What had possessed him to kiss Vee Bishop? Talk about a gigantic step in the wrong direction.

Not that he regretted kissing Vee. At that second, and even now as he thought about it, he had very much wanted to kiss her. He still did.

He just *shouldn't* have.

Kissing Vee complicated every part of his life. It wasn't anything a cup of coffee could cure, but he thought going to Cup o' Jo was a good first step. Maybe Jo would have some good advice for him, or perhaps a jolt of caffeine might set him straight, though he highly doubted it.

What did a man do when he was headed down the wrong road? He'd made a mess of this whole thing. Vee might never speak to him again.

And then he had Veronica Jayne to consider. He'd only just sent her his picture. She might interpret that to mean something more than it was, which of course he hadn't considered until after he sent the photograph. What if she thought he was leading her on?

He'd made that mistake in the past with women, and whatever happened, he didn't want to hurt Veronica Jayne. She was special to him, and he cared for her, even if it was something completely different than what he felt for Vee.

He was no longer caught up in wondering what Veronica Jayne really looked like, and he wasn't madly checking his email to see if she'd sent her photograph. He simply didn't feel for her the way he felt for Vee, even if he was unable to put words to exactly what his feelings for Vee were.

Honestly, the last thing he should have been doing was pursuing a relationship with *any* woman right now. He could not be in a less-stable position than he was at this moment—in a transition phase on his way to mission work. That was his calling. He couldn't just drop it and suddenly become the kind of man Vee would want in her life.

Not that he knew what kind of man Vee wanted, or if she wanted a man at all. The truth was, he had no idea how Vee felt about what had happened between them, other than the fact that she had freaked out and run away.

And that wasn't exactly a good sign, was it?

He'd definitely caught her off-guard. He'd caught *himself* off-guard.

What was he going to say if he had to talk to her? Obviously, he would have to talk to her. Eventually. He wasn't a man of words. He preferred action—only in this case, it was *action* that had gotten him in trouble.

With an inward sigh, Ben entered Cup o' Jo and walked up to the counter to order a double espresso—the strongest thing they served.

As always, Jo was behind the counter waiting on customers. She was always about, setting the tone of the café to be like a second home to her customers and friends. She made everyone feel welcome, and no matter what kind of day Ben was having, she always managed to make him feel better.

Jo had a never-ending set of interesting T-shirts, a different one every day of the week. Today her shirt proclaimed If It's Broke, Fix It.

Ben frowned. That was definitely a skewed version of the old cliché.

Jo set his cup of coffee before him with a speculative look on her face. She was only quiet for a second before speaking her mind.

"Did you fix things, dear?" she asked bluntly.

Ben raised a brow. "I'm sorry—fix what?"

Jo shook her purple dishtowel at him. "You know perfectly well what I'm talking about. Between you and Vee. I could tell there was something going on there. First you take off after her during the carnival. You didn't even bother to dry yourself off with a towel. Now, I don't mind one whit that you called me in to help with Nigel and Felix yesterday, but if you think you're keeping me in the dark with what's happening between you and Vee, you've got another thing coming."

Ben downed his espresso in two gulps and choked on the bitter aftertaste.

"Well, did you get a chance to talk to her?" Jo was nothing if not straightforward to a fault.

Ben's face flamed. *Talking* wasn't exactly what happened between him and Vee. Not that he would tell Jo that.

"A little bit," he answered vaguely.

Jo leaned over the counter and tapped him on the shoulder with a closed fist. "Well, then, talk a little bit more, son. Make the effort. I promise she will be worth it."

What was she talking about? Despite the fact that Jo was like a second mother to him—or maybe because of that—he definitely did not like the feeling that the woman was inside his head.

He slid the mug over the counter without meeting Jo's gaze. Maybe if he didn't quite look at her...

"Thanks for the brew," he said, turning away so she wouldn't see the confusion and angst in his eyes. Clearly she was reading something into nothing—or was that nothing into something?

Spinning around turned out to be an even greater problem because Vee had just walked in the door with Olivia. They were both dressed in sweats and running shoes. Vee's hair was in a ponytail, not a bun, which startled Ben. The swing of her hair made her look so—*feminine.* She'd clearly been working out—her face was flushed and wisps of hair that had escaped her ponytail framed her heart-shaped face—yet she looked so lovely, all ruffled and not quite put together.

His heart jumped into his throat. She noticed

him just seconds after the moment he saw her. Their gazes locked and held while Ben's mind spun wildly, searching for the right words to say in the singularly most awkward moment of his life.

"Hey, Vee. Olivia."

So smooth. Cary Grant could take lessons from him. If he could have slapped himself upside the head without anyone noticing, he would have.

"Did you enjoy the carnival?" Olivia teased, picking up the conversation and running with it. "I heard the water was nice and cold."

Ben could almost see the layers upon layers of emotional barriers going up around Vee.

Obstacles he didn't know how to cross.

He made a choking noise. Clearly, he wasn't able to *fix* the problem at all. He didn't have the vaguest notion how women thought.

He tried to look nonchalant, to force casual words from his lips. He really did. But there was nothing there. His head was whirling and his thoughts were screaming and he knew if he didn't leave that moment, he would make an utter fool of himself.

"Ladies," he rumbled from deep in his throat. He planted his cowboy hat on his head, tipped it to them with a nod and tried very hard not to run as he passed by them, heading for the exit and the fresh air he so desperately needed.

A man had to breathe, after all. And around Vee Bishop, that was impossible to do.

"He did *what?*" Olivia screeched, reaching for Vee's elbow and shaking her with great enthusiasm.

"Can you please lower your voice?" Vee whispered coarsely. "In case you didn't notice, Ben is sitting right across the room from us." Ben had stepped out of the café for a moment, but now he was seated in the back corner opposite her, slumped behind a computer screen.

Olivia snickered. "Oh, I noticed, all right. It was hard not to, with you two acting all weird around each other."

"Can you please, *please* not make a big deal out of this? You are going to make me sorry I told you anything." Vee buried her head in her hands.

"Oh, like you could keep something as monumental as this from me. Not going to happen. I already knew something was brewing between you and Ben, but I had no idea the soup was done. How long have you two been an item? Was it just after the carnival or have you been keeping it under wraps for longer than that?"

"You have the oddest metaphors," Vee commented, chuckling despite the fact that her best friend was putting her on the spot. "I'm begging you not to make this—" she paused slightly "—*episode* into more than it is. Ben and I are *not* a couple, nor do I think we ever will be."

Olivia lifted a brow. "Really?"

"If we were—and I'm not saying that's even a possibility—you'd be the first to know."

"I want to hear details. Play-by-play, girl. I want to know it all. I'm still in shock to learn that he kissed you."

"*You're* in shock," Vee responded with a groan. "I'm completely stunned. I don't know *how* it happened, let alone *why*."

"Well, duh. I know why."

"How fortunate for you," Vee replied dryly. "You were there at the carnival when Jo suggested that I win a date with Ben if I dunked him, right?"

"Oh, yes. And you *sooo* dunked him." Olivia laughed. "People are still talking about it. Adding ten feet to your throw. That was pure genius, Vee. Pure genius. Everybody thought so."

"Everybody but Ben. My actions were foolish, that's what they were. I left right afterward, and then I started feeling badly about the way I've been treating him, especially back at the dunking booth. I wanted to apologize to him, but I wasn't ready to talk to him when he came chasing after me. I hadn't even prayed about it."

"Dunking Ben wasn't a big deal, hon. I'm sure he doesn't hold it against you."

"Maybe not, but don't you agree that I ended up humiliating him in front of all of our friends? I made such a big deal about *not* going out with him that it made it seem like I thought he was a bad guy, someone I would never date. How awful was that?"

"It was only because you were flustered. And you had good intentions, even when you were turning Ben away. You were thinking of me, being loyal to me. That's a good character trait when taken in context. Surely he understood that when you explained it all to him."

Vee's face flamed and she choked on her coffee.

"We didn't exactly get to that part."

"So are you telling me he just dashed up from behind, whirled you around and planted one on you? How incredibly romantic." Olivia sighed deeply, resting her chin on her palm. Her gaze turned dreamy. In Vee's opinion, Olivia was enjoying this whole situation far too much for her liking.

"How *appalling,* you mean. I can't even look him in the eye. And just in case you hadn't noticed, he's clearly avoiding me, too. It's pretty obvious that he thinks that kissing me was the wrong thing to do. It was a mistake that never should have happened."

"There is nothing at all obvious happening here. You're reading way too much into his every single move. He may look like a big lug, but Ben is a very sensitive man, Vee. He feels deeply, but he doesn't always show it. You know how guys are. They keep everything locked inside. I have a good notion that he's infatuated with you and isn't sure what his next move should be. I mean really, how do you follow a dramatic kiss like he gave you?"

"I haven't a clue."

"Maybe he's just giving you space to process what happened. Maybe he's getting his nerve up to ask you on a proper date."

Vee inhaled deeply and darted a glance at Ben. His gaze was squarely on the computer screen in front of him.

How did she feel about all that had happened? Did she dare put a name to it? Label or classify it? Where, exactly, were her emotions pointing when it came to Ben Atwood?

And more to the point, how did *he* feel about her?

Awkward.

That's how Ben was feeling. Completely out of his depth.

He slunk down a little lower in his seat, wishing he could disappear or at least find a way to get out of the café without having to pass by Vee again. He was still staring at an empty computer screen. When he'd sat down to write an email, he'd come up blank. He'd quickly decided that soliciting advice from Veronica Jayne was a bad idea. He didn't want to hurt her feelings.

That said, he didn't know *what* to do.

It was almost as if he were in high school again, getting flustered when the girl he liked walked past. Only this wasn't high school, and he'd already *kissed* the girl he liked.

He didn't know whether that was an act of courage or flagrant foolishness. He'd sought God's will, but so far had come up empty-handed. If the Lord was directing him, he must be missing the clues.

He had his life here in Serendipity, but his dreams and his future lay in stateside mission work. His attraction to Vee Bishop grew stronger every day, but what good could come from that?

She was too intense and independent a woman to expect her to change her plans to suit him, and he wasn't the kind of man who could leave his wife behind at home while he was off doing mission work. And that was assuming his attraction to her was reciprocated at all.

She *had* kissed him back—he was positive of that. Actually, she'd more or less initiated the kiss. But he could analyze the moment to death and never figure out how she felt about him.

Then there was Veronica Jayne, his mystery flower girl. He held no illusions now that they could try to date—not with the strength of his feelings for Vee. But he still hoped that he and Veronica Jayne could remain friends after their class was done.

He'd been praying and praying that he would someday be as strong on the inside as he was on the outside, but spiritual growth was a lot more difficult than physical growth. Building muscles on his biceps and chest was a cakewalk compared to trying to sort out his current emotions.

The one thing that he did know was that he was falling for Vee—hard. He didn't know whether she returned the sentiment, and he definitely didn't know how God would have Vee fit into his future, but there it was in black and white.

Now he needed to make a plan and make it work. Vee wasn't going to make this easy on him. For one thing, she was completely immune to his charm, or whatever it was that other women saw in him. She wasn't flirtatious like they were—not that he knew what to do with a flirtatious woman any more than he knew what to do with a scrupulously unsociable one.

How could a man feel so completely hopeless and yet utterly hopeful at the same time?

Only a woman could do that to a man.

One woman. Vee.

Ben wiggled the computer mouse to bring the screen to light again. He opened his email account and quickly scanned down the list, wondering if he'd find the familiar moniker that usually awaited him.

Veronica Jayne.

Except there was no email from Veronica Jayne. Not a word and not a picture.

Had he scared her away by pushing their friendship forward too quickly? Had he shaken her up by sending her his picture?

It figured. He was somehow managing to make a mess of *all* the relationships in his life.

It just figured. With a growl of frustration, he closed the browser and stalked out of the café without so much as a backward glance.

"Did you ever check your email to see if BJ sent you a picture?" Olivia queried with a sly smile that bespoke more than a little curiosity.

"I thought you were trying to get me to see

the good side of Ben Atwood. I can't do that and worry about BJ at the same time. Not that I'm admitting to feeling anything for Ben, mind you."

"Of course you're not. You're going to be as muleheaded about Ben as you always are with everything. And just so we're clear, my main goal in life right now is to make you see that Ben is a good man and deserving of a chance. But that said, it never hurts to have a backup plan, don't you think?"

Vee felt like Olivia had pushed her in the chest.

A backup plan? Is that was BJ was?

If she was being honest, she had to admit that he might have been so, at least at some point. Perhaps that's what he always had been, the guy she'd had in her cyber back pocket in case the real thing—a face-to-face relationship with a man—never materialized.

But now Ben was in the picture, whatever that meant, and she and BJ were talking about exchanging pictures. This was all getting far too real for her and far too complicated for her liking. Sure, they'd talked about meeting each other at a stateside mission someday, but that *day* had always been some distant, unspecified date in the future.

She had mixed feelings about the whole thing.

Half of her was scared to death to see what BJ looked like. The other half didn't really care at all—because, to be honest, her heart was leaning elsewhere. What did it matter what BJ did or did not look like when she couldn't keep her mind off Ben?

Her heart roared in her ears. She definitely wasn't ready for *that* kind of honesty yet. She couldn't even look Ben in the eye. That did not bode well for any kind of real relationship with Ben, but no matter what happened on that front, she knew without a doubt that she could never have any kind of a relationship with BJ while she felt this way about another man.

It saddened her to think there would be no more emails to look forward to, no more bright spots in her day just knowing BJ was out there somewhere, possibly thinking of her just the way she had been thinking of him.

As a friend. A supporter. He'd definitely been those things.

She sighed. What was the old proverb? All good things must come to an end? She supposed that applied to mythical internet relationships, too.

"Hello? Earth to Vee. Are you reading, Vee?"

"Huh?" Vee snapped out of her reverie to find Olivia waving a hand in front of her face.

"That's what I thought. You aren't paying any attention to me at all. You're staring at Ben."

She snapped her gaze back to Olivia's. "Was not."

"Were, too. Deny it all you want, girlfriend, but you've got a thing for him."

"I thought we were talking about BJ."

Olivia barked out a laugh. "Did anyone ever tell you how contrary you are? When I mention Ben, you want to talk about BJ. When I suggest we see what the elusive BJ looks like, you want to talk about Ben."

"I am not contrary," she countered, then realized that simply by answering she was proving Olivia's point.

"So you'll check your email to see if BJ sent his picture? And you'll look at it if he did?"

"You aren't going to let this go, are you?" Vee muttered morosely.

"Have you ever known me to let go of an interesting tidbit of gossip?"

"This isn't gossip."

"No, it is not. It is *way* better than gossip. More interesting, by far," Olivia assured her.

"Fine," Vee snapped.

"Fine? You mean you'll look at the photograph?"

"No. I mean *you'll* look if it's that interesting to you. I don't even want to know what BJ looks like anymore."

"Because you've already fallen for Ben."

Vee sighed dramatically. "Do you know that you exasperate me sometimes?"

Olivia grinned like the Cheshire cat. "I know. And you love me for it."

"Actually, I love you in spite of it, if you must know."

Olivia reached in front of Vee and wiggled the computer mouse, bringing the screen in front of the two of them to light.

Vee's stomach clenched as she opened up the webpage for her email, then typed in her password to pull up her new messages. Maybe BJ hadn't written. Or maybe he hadn't sent a photograph like he'd said he was going to.

She glanced at the screen and sighed. Sure enough, there was a message from BJ, complete with an attachment.

She really, *really* was not ready for this. There was no way she was opening his letter. Not now, at least. She hovered the pointer over the *X* that would close the browser.

"Oh, no you don't," Olivia reprimanded, laying a hand over hers. She really was pushy when she wanted something, Vee thought sullenly. This was one time that she didn't appreciate that character trait in her best friend.

"I can't do this." She knew Olivia wouldn't buy it, but she had to try to sell it nonetheless.

"Fine." Olivia's tone was a cross between enjoyment and exasperation. Mostly amusement, bless her heart. "Then I'll do it for you. Scoot over and hand me that mouse."

Vee thought about arguing, but what was the point? Besides, if she deleted the email without looking at BJ's photo, there would be a teeny, tiny part of her that would always wonder what she'd missed. Olivia was right. Seeing BJ's photograph would offer her a measure of closure so she could go on with her life. That said…

"I can't look." Vee braced her elbows on the table and pushed her palms against her eyes, completely darkening her vision. "Promise that you won't keep me in suspense too long," she squeaked. "Just take a quick look at the man and put me out of my misery."

"No problem. I'll fill you in on the general details, and then you can decide if you want to have a peek yourself. I'll give you all the good stuff. You know what I'm talking about. Tall. Short. Big. Little. Handsome. Troll."

"Olivia!"

"Kidding. I'm kidding. No, not really. I'm not. Who better than me to discern if a man is right for you? Your best friend since kindergarten. I know you better than anyone. I'll point you in the right direction."

"You're pushing Ben at me," Vee felt led to point out.

"Exactly."

With her elbows braced on the table and her palms tightly covering her eyes, she heard, rather than saw, the abrupt change in Olivia's demeanor as her best friend swept in a high, squeaky breath and exclaimed in surprise.

"Oh, my. Oh my, oh my, oh my."

Vee groaned and pushed her palms more tightly against her eyes, as if that would somehow make this situation go away. "What is it? Does he have scales?"

"Um, not exactly," Olivia answered slowly. "No, I definitely would not say that."

"What, then? Is he a modern-day replica of Clark Gable, so unbelievably gorgeous that he instantly took your breath away and made your heart leap out of your chest?"

Vee expected Olivia to break into laughter at her measly attempt at humor, but she sounded surprisingly sober for one who had only moments earlier been pushing Vee to take a look at her mystery man.

The mood had changed. Vee felt it in every fiber of her being. Every muscle tensed, every tendon stretched, until she was shaking from the effort of merely being there.

"You're getting warmer," Olivia offered after a painful pause.

"Well, that's good to know," Vee replied, as tongue-in-cheek as she could manage. "So he's not dreadful to look at, then?"

"Not at all." *That* answer came quickly. Maybe too quickly.

"So describe him to me. I'm dying here."

"You could just look."

"I could, but why spoil your fun?" Actually, Vee was still battling her own fear. It wouldn't help her to stretch it out any more than necessary, but she couldn't help but try.

"Okay, then." Olivia started out slowly, drawing out each syllable. "Broad shoulders, dark hair, nice eyes."

"Nice eyes? That's kind of vague, don't you think? What color are they?"

"They're kind of a mixture of colors. They're hard to describe with words. You'll just have to open your eyes and see for yourself. And Vee? Leaving personality aside, and past history, who is the best-looking man in Serendipity?"

Vee felt the tension leave her shoulders. Olivia was obviously talking about Ben. If BJ was anywhere near as handsome as Ben At-wood, Vee had nothing to fear in looking at his picture, except the terrifying notion of him ever finding out what *she* looked like.

Boy, would he be disappointed. But that was not going to happen, since she had no intention of sending him a picture back—especially now that she'd learned BJ was a handsome man—it was all good.

"Vee?" Olivia queried. "You didn't answer my question."

"Ben. Ben Atwood. He's the best-looking man in town," she said, low enough that others nearby would not overhear. "I know that's what you think, too. So does BJ look like Ben, then?"

"Yeah, about that." Olivia hesitated again.

"Well, does he?"

"Yes. Yes, he definitely looks like Ben."

Vee did *not* like the way Olivia's voice sounded, all high and squeaky and strangled. An awful possibility filled Vee's mind to explain why she was having such difficulty.

Ready to face the truth at last, or at least unable to deny it any longer, she dropped her hands from her eyes, already knowing what she was going to see when she looked at the screen.

Or rather, *who.*

"No way," she croaked, shaking her head fervently.

No. Possible. Way.

"This cannot be happening to me. Olivia, there must be some kind of mistake."

"Think of the odds," Olivia agreed, sounding as astounded as Vee felt.

Ben Atwood, staring out at her with his easy, charming half smile, his luminous bronze-green eyes—the ones no words could adequately describe—making her heart roar in her ears until she could hardly hear anything else.

Vee couldn't process it. She just couldn't.

"Ben can't be BJ," Vee hissed in a harsh whisper, desperately leaning toward Olivia's shoulder, half for support and half so that she would not be overheard. "Turn off that traitorous machine before someone else sees his picture on there! This is not right. There must be some kind of horrible mistake."

"Like what, Vee? How would BJ get his hands on a picture of Ben unless he *is* Ben?"

"I don't know, but there must be some other explanation. Something. Anything."

She knew that there wasn't another explanation for this phenomenon, just as deeply and absolutely as the fact that she hadn't had a *single clue* that BJ was Ben before this very moment.

How could she have worked with him every day, held conversations, even kissed him, and *not known?* It was unfathomable.

"Maybe there's another man in this town,"

Olivia suggested, "using Ben's picture because he's the better-looking one. Maybe he's trying to pass himself off as Ben because he's really as ugly as a rock."

"It's not another man in Serendipity," Vee admitted with a groan. "Anyway, BJ could never be ugly to me, no matter what he looked like."

Ben. Not BJ. That would take some time to process.

"No, it's doubtless *not* another man. I'm sorry, Vee, but I can't think of any other scenarios, probable or otherwise. So what are you going to do about it, now that you know it's Ben on the other end of the line?"

She wanted to scream, but she was in public. Maybe later, into her pillow at home.

"*Do* about it?" she whispered weakly, hardly able to speak. "I don't know."

Her heart sunk. What *was* she going to do about it?

"You have to do something."

"No I don't," Vee replied just a bit too quickly. "I don't have to do anything about it at all. I can simply delete the email and pretend I never saw Ben's picture. Simple as that. End of story."

"Really? You think you can do that?" Olivia peered at her speculatively and then shook her head. "You think you can just pretend it never happened, that you never discovered that BJ and Ben were one and the same? Do you think you can work alongside Ben every day and never give away any indication that you and he were ever a cyber-item? And what about your class with BJ? Aren't you working on a project together?"

"You make it sound impossible," Vee complained grumpily. Which, of course, it was. Even if she could ignore Ben in person, she could hardly ignore BJ. Half his grade was their combined project. She took the computer mouse away from Olivia, who hadn't yet closed the browser. Not only was Vee afraid someone else might see the telling photograph, but she simply couldn't stand to look directly at Ben's smiling face a moment longer.

No wonder Olivia couldn't describe the color of Ben's eyes. They defied explanation, at least any kind that could be put into words.

"Honestly, I think it would be impossible. I know I couldn't do it, even if I tried. I'd be bound to slip up eventually and say something that would tip him off."

That was Olivia, though, who, bless her soul, tended to chatter. Vee was more hush-hush about things. She'd more than likely be able to pull it off.

Except for the fact that she'd blush to her toes

every time her eyes met Ben's, and how obvious was that? Vee wasn't a blushing woman any more than she was a talkative one, so her turning the color of an apple at inopportune moments would be a dead giveaway.

Oh, what was she going to do?

"Maybe you could just send him your picture back? Throw the ball into his court and let him decide what to do with it? If nothing else, he'd be able to experience the same shock you are feeling."

Vee thought that was an excellent suggestion, for about one second, until she started thinking about the ramifications of such an act.

First of all, she'd have to find a photograph to send him, and she did *not* take good pictures. Not that it mattered, but she had her pride. Second, the wait would be excruciating. She'd be on pins and needles every second after she hit Send.

And what if he decided never to speak to her about it at all? Could she really handle working around him and seeing him around town knowing that he knew that she knew that...

This was getting *really* complicated.

Impossible, more like.

Why had she ever, *ever* thought she could conduct any sort of relationship online, romantic or otherwise? Had she really believed it would somehow be easier than conducting her affairs in person?

The whole situation would have been funny if it wasn't so serious. She certainly wasn't laughing now.

"Maybe you should just come clean with him," Olivia suggested. "Just tell him the truth—that you were surprised to learn it was him when you received his picture, and you're sure he'll be as flabbergasted as you to discover you've each been emailing someone who lives in the same town—who works for the same fire department, to be exact."

"That's going to go over well." Vee couldn't even imagine how she would start *that* conversation.

"Maybe you two will eventually laugh about it," Olivia suggested.

"Somehow I don't think he'll find this funny." Not any more than she did. He'd probably think it was much, much worse.

She was on the winning end of this equation. Plain Jayne meets Hunky Paramedic. No contest there.

Yeah, no. That wasn't going to happen. She could not stand the humiliation of coming clean on this one.

"Remember, he did kiss you," Olivia reminded

her, as if she had somehow deduced where Vee's thoughts had taken her.

That was true. Vee wondered how she'd forgotten about Ben's kiss, even for a moment. Technically, she'd kissed him, but he hadn't seemed to mind.

Which only served to complicate matters even further, if that were possible.

She didn't know how to feel about what had happened between them, only that she'd been surprised at the intense feelings he stirred in her. She'd always thought she disliked him, putting it mildly; and maybe she had because of what he'd done to Olivia.

But now she'd let that go. And that she *was* attracted to him, though she had initially tried to deny it.

Given that new bit of insight, there was no way bringing the current situation to light would be a good idea for anyone involved. Heartache, maybe even heartbreak, was the very best she could hope for.

But what else could she do?

Delete her email account?

No, she'd still have to work with Ben. And she couldn't leave BJ in the lurch without finishing her end of the project. Different solution, same problems.

Quit the fire station?

How was that fair? Because she knew about the online relationship and he didn't? That just didn't seem right.

Maybe she should just pack up and move.

To Siberia.

To be a tiger trainer.

She thought that was her best idea yet. Out of sight, out of mind and out of country.

If only it were that easy.

"What am I going to do?" she groaned to Olivia. It was a rhetorical question, obviously, with no answer whatsoever, and she'd already asked it several times this afternoon.

There was no more time to think about it. The high-pitched *beep, beep, beep* of her emergency pager broke into her thoughts.

She was needed at the firehouse. There was some kind of emergency situation.

Her problems with Ben would have to wait.

She had a job to do.

Chapter Twelve

Ben was already at the station when the call came through, so he was a first-responder to the location. According to the operator, a leak in a gas stove had caused an explosion in the kitchen of a farmhouse a couple of miles south of Serendipity. The whole unstable house was coming down at an alarming rate.

As with nearly all of the emergencies in the tri-county area, Ben knew the folks involved. The Salingers were part of Ben's church family. They had four children under ten—two boys ages six and nine, a three-year-old little girl and an infant son.

Ben's adrenaline was pumping full steam ahead as he hit the siren to the ambulance and flipped the switch for the flashing lights, even knowing his skills as a paramedic would probably not be needed. The neighbor who'd called it in said the family had gotten out of the blaze safely and were standing by for assistance.

He was more worried about the structure of the old farmhouse itself and the way its loss would affect the family. The Salingers must be terrified and heartbroken as they watched their home burn to the ground. Ben sent up a quick prayer thanking God for the Salingers' safety and asked Him to watch over them and comfort them in their time of need.

Vee was standing near the back of the fire truck just ahead of him, her right arm looped around a spit-shined silver handle made exactly for that purpose. Her face looked serious underneath the wide width of her helmet. Her brow was low and her jaw was set. As always, the woman meant business.

Ben gripped the steering wheel harder. He had the eeriest feeling that she was looking directly at him. That there was a question in her eyes that she was expecting him to answer.

And how unlikely was that? He was starting to imagine emotions where there weren't any. Going mental, and all over a woman.

Sure, they both needed to confront their issues with each other, but now was definitely not the time to do so, and she knew it as well as he did. Thinking she was staring at him was all in his head.

He averted his gaze and concentrated on the road before him. Zach Bowden, sitting beside him, tapped a pencil against the clipboard he was holding and then tucked the writing utensil behind his ear. Usually his partner had something witty to say to lighten the mood. Often he'd describe humorous or entertainingly dramatic situations he'd encountered with his wife or his children.

Today he was unusually silent. He'd obviously been Ben's partner long enough to realize something was amiss. He noticed Zach giving him several speculative sidelong glances.

Zach, however, wasn't the type to stay silent for long. Somehow Ben knew that when Zach finally spoke, it wouldn't be a tale about something his family had gone through recently.

"Are you okay, buddy?" Zach finally asked. "Did you ever get a photograph back from that—what's her name? Veronica Jayne?"

Ben didn't answer, choosing instead to keep his attention on driving.

"So that's how it's going to be, is it? I guess your silence is all I need to know to answer my own question. I can clearly see that your mind is elsewhere."

"I'm fine," Ben ground out, exasperated by his partner's incessant prying. Guys weren't supposed to have these kinds of conversations. Zach had been married too long.

His answer was probably fudging the truth a little bit. He really wasn't *fine*. Ben knew that Zach wanted a real answer, not just the off-the-cuff reply he'd given him, but that was all Ben had to offer right now.

"And?" Zach prodded.

"No, I have not received an email from Veronica Jayne, not that being fine and receiving word from Veronica Jayne are in any way related. And the reason my mind is elsewhere is because I'm praying for the Salingers."

"And not at all because Vee Bishop is currently in your direct line of vision?"

Ben was glad it was dark so that Zach couldn't see him color. He knew that the warm flush to his face would have him cherry-red by now.

Zach chuckled as if he could see Ben's discomfiture. "That's what I thought. You and your lady problems. I knew you were a little off your game tonight. Delia and I went through some rough patches, too, but now look at us, happily married with two beautiful sons. It can't get any better than that, partner."

Ben didn't bother trying to point out to Zach that a couple could only experience a rough patch if they were a *couple* to begin with.

Besides, he didn't want to talk about Vee.

"Can we pray for the Salingers?" he suggested, not entirely for the right reasons but close enough. "Out loud?"

By the time the fire tanker pulled up to the burning house, the scene was absolute chaos. The police had been called to the scene, and they had their hands full trying to contain the crowd. Some folks were there for the sake of the family, and others strained for a decent view of the fire, one of the most exciting things to happen in months.

It was amazing how quickly word spread in Serendipity. Half the town must be there. There weren't many true emergencies in town, and Vee knew folks in general tended to be oddly drawn to such tragedy and trauma.

Most, out of the goodness of their hearts, were there to try to help the Salingers however they could, but attempting to maintain crowd control when the fire department was trying to fight a fire only added to their responsibilities.

Vee caught her police-officer brother Eli's eye and nodded a quick greeting before turning to her work. Every person on the detail had a specific job to do. Chief Jenkins shouted orders while some of the men hooked up the fire hose to the tanker and began blasting the low-level flames.

Vee's job was a little less physical but equally as important as fighting the fire with water. She was the firefighter in charge of assessing the scene. First, she had to ascertain that all the people and animals who might have been in the building were safe and clear of the edifice. After that, she'd evaluate the fire itself, both in terms of the extent of the flames and the possible structural damages to the house.

Unfortunately, in Serendipity, where many folks still lived in primarily clapboard houses, structural damage was the rule and not the exception. Vee anticipated that the house would quickly be completely consumed in flames given the magnitude of this particular blaze.

She'd make a thorough tour of the fire site as soon as she was able, and then she'd make a report back to Chief Jenkins, but first she needed to find the Salingers and make sure they were all safe and unharmed. Ben and Zach were waiting at the site in case anyone needed any kind of medical assistance.

Between the dark of the moonless night and the amount of smoke pouring out of the building, it was difficult to see the nose in front of her face, much less figure out where the Salinger family was amid the enormous group of Serendipity locals.

Suddenly Vee heard someone scream, a fierce shriek that cut through the murky air like a knife, stabbing Vee right in the gut. She turned in the direction of the sound and began running, peering to the right and left of her to see if she could locate the source of the noise through the billowing smoke.

A distraught Emma Salinger forced her way through the crowd and ran into Vee's arms, nearly plowing her over. She grasped Vee's jacket and yanked hard on it, urging her toward the burning house.

"My baby, my baby, my baby, my baby," she repeated over and over, shaking Vee with every syllable. Emma had a frenzied look in her eye.

"Emma," Vee stated firmly, making sure she was loud enough to be heard over the din of the crowd, the trucks, Chief Jenkins barking out orders and the firemen shouting information to one another. "Look at me. Honey. Emma. Look. At. Me."

The hysterical woman only cried louder. "My baby! My baby!"

Vee's mind was spinning. Had the infant somehow been left inside the house when everyone had evacuated the premises?

"Where is Preston?" Vee asked.

Kent Salinger appeared at Vee's elbow, his infant son tucked protectively into his shoulder.

"Here's the baby," he answered for his frantic wife. "Honey, Preston is right here. Everything is going to be all right."

Vee gritted her teeth. How could he even say that? They were safe, but the Salingers had no place to call home anymore.

"No," Emma insisted, ignoring her husband and gripping Vee's jacket with renewed fervor. "No. Not Preston. It's Crystal."

Crystal, their three-year-old daughter.

"She's not with you?" Kent asked, starting to sound as panic-stricken as his wife.

"She was," Emma admitted and then crumbled to the ground. "She was with me. Dear God, save her."

Vee followed the woman down, crouching before her. "Emma, where is your daughter?"

"She ran back in the house." Emma choked on a sob. "Calliope was in there. I couldn't stop her."

"Who is Calliope?" Vee asked, confused.

"Crystal's favorite doll," Kent answered over his shoulder. The man had already slid Preston into Emma's weak arms and was at a dead run for what was left of the front door of the house.

Vee's pulse roared in her ears as her adrenaline burst through her veins. The entire house was engulfed in flames. Kent was crazy if he thought he could survive entering the dwelling with no protective clothing or training in dealing with fires. He'd never make it out alive, much less rescue his daughter.

Vee dashed forward and dived for Kent, hitting him behind the knees and knocking him squarely to the ground with a jolt so hard it knocked the wind out of her and probably out of him, too. Kent was already struggling underneath her, trying to get away.

"Let me go," he screamed, thrashing his legs. "I've got to get Crystal."

His heel met Vee on the chin and she was knocked flat on her back. Though she could see the gush of blood that poured down the front of her jacket, she could not feel the pain.

"Kent," she screamed at him, grabbing at one leg. "You can't do this. Let me. I'm trained for this. Trust me. I *will* get your daughter out safely."

Or die trying.

Chief Jenkins appeared at her side and wrestled Kent to a standing position, keeping a firm hand around his upper arm. Ben rushed forward to grasp Kent's other arm. Chief and Ben were both large men, and though Kent tried, he could not break the firefighters' combined grip.

"You're bleeding, Vee," Ben said.

"It's nothing but a superficial cut." She wiped her chin with the back of her palm.

Vee knew this was her moment. She wasn't wearing her SBCA gear, the tank and mask that would allow her to be able to breathe in the inferno. Her duties this evening, liaising with the family and the community and assessing structural issues, shouldn't have required her to carry the heavy equipment around, so she'd elected not to gear up with them. It had never been an issue before, and she hadn't thought twice about it.

She was thinking about it now.

She had a decision to make and no time to make it in. It was now or never. She had to save that little girl.

Taking one last glance back at the rest of the Salinger family, who were huddling together crying for their daughter and sister, she pressed her visor down over her face and dashed for the building.

She could hear Chief Jenkins yelling at her to come back, heard him issue her a direct order *not* to enter the building. The structure was caving in. It wasn't safe for anyone to dare a rescue, especially without the proper breathing apparatus.

Vee knew that despite the odds, Chief Jenkins would have organized a team to try to save little Crystal, but by then it would be too late. The entire house was already engulfed in flames. She couldn't live with herself if she didn't at least try.

Chief would be furious when she returned, and she would no doubt be suspended from the force for her actions, and rightly so, but she would deal with those ramifications afterward, when Crystal Salinger was safe. Her mind was entirely focused on getting in and getting herself and that girl out of that house alive.

Just before she plunged through what was left of the front door, she heard Ben's voice calling to her, a terrified bellow that was halfway between horror and rage.

"Vee! Vee-ee!" His deep, tinny voice echoed through her consciousness at what seemed to be an unimaginable distance, but she could not stop now. Not with a little girl's life on the line.

As soon as she broke through the door, she immediately dropped to her hands and knees, crawling to avoid the worst of the smoke. Her lungs already burned, and she knew she wouldn't survive long without her breathing apparatus. She tugged the top of her collar over her nose and gritted her teeth, trying not to breathe any more than was necessary.

Her firefighter training kicked in full force, right along with her adrenaline, as she scrambled toward what she hoped was the little girl's bedroom. She was working off of zero information. She didn't know when the girl had entered the building, or where, or where she might have thought to have gone after she'd entered the house.

"Crystal! Crystal!" She tried calling the girl's name, but with her collar muffling her voice and the fire roaring around her she knew the three-year-old would never be able to hear her. She couldn't see her hands in front of her face because of the flames and the billowing smoke. The poor girl must be terrified, assuming she was still conscious. She might have passed out already. Vee wouldn't even consider the alternative.

She moved as close to the sides of the room as she dared, feeling her way forward. She didn't want the walls to cave in on her, but she needed the structure to guide her through the house. This was a shot in the dark, grasping forward and to her sides and hoping beyond hope that her gloved hand would meet the little girl's body.

Vee prayed frantically as she methodically swept one room and then a second. She knew she didn't have much time left to get out of the house before it came down around her. The girl had even less, having been exposed to the smoke for a longer period.

Just inside the third bedroom she thought she heard a small whimper.

Was she imagining it? Did she want to find little Crystal so badly that her ears were hearing sounds that did not exist?

No. She heard it again. Directly in front of her. A terrified little squeak, not much more than a murmur. How Vee even heard it over the roar of the fire was nothing short of a gift from God.

Vee scrambled forward, almost falling over the little girl, who was huddled in a small ball in the center of the room, her arms tucked over her head and a little rag doll with red yarn for hair poking out from between her knees.

Vee knew her firefighter's uniform might frighten the already terrified little girl. Lifting her visor was risky, but she'd already gone about as far out on a limb as was possible, anyway. It would be far less difficult to get them both out alive if the child wasn't fighting her every step of the way.

"Crystal," Vee shouted, not wanting to scare the girl but needing for her to be able to hear. "My name is Vee. I know you're scared, honey, but I'm here to get you and Calliope back to your mommy and daddy, okay?"

The little girl nodded and clutched her doll to her chest.

Vee wrapped Crystal's arms around her neck and grasped her wrists with one hand.

"We're going to take a little horsey ride, okay, honey? You just hold on tight and I'll get you out of here."

Crystal wasn't heavy or awkward to carry. With all the adrenaline coursing through Vee, she could barely feel the girl's weight at all. Vee crawled on her knees with her one free hand, heading straight back to the one opening she knew would be her best opportunity for breaking free of the house.

It seemed an eternity before she could make out the shape of the front door. A couple of times her grip slipped on the little girl's wrists and she'd had to stop and readjust Crystal's position on her shoulders. Her lungs burned from the smoke and from holding her breath. She could only imagine how the little girl felt.

Chief had evidently ordered a couple of the men to widen the doorway with their axes, so she didn't have to worry about either one of them being snagged by any protruding pieces of wood.

They were almost there. Almost…there…

And then they'd made it. Two firefighters met

her just inside the door to help her scramble the final few feet out of the entranceway.

The moment they were free of the door, Zach gently took Crystal from her and carried the child to the ambulance, where her family anxiously awaited.

Vee didn't even realize she was still crawling on her hands and knees until her gloved palms slipped out from underneath her on the wet grass. She sprawled to the earth, taking sweeping gasps of air, though it was still acrid with smoke. It was better, at least, than what she'd been facing in the building.

It was only through God's grace that she and the child had made it out alive.

"Thank you, Jesus," she said aloud as she groaned and rolled over onto her back. Even though she was lying flat on the ground, her vision blurred and her head spun in dizzy waves. Every muscle in her body ached as if she'd been pummeled in a boxing ring, especially her chin where Kent Salinger had kicked her. The adrenaline was fading, and she could feel the pain of it now.

She closed her eyes, trying to steady herself, searching for the willpower to roll to a sitting position. She was in enough trouble as it was, even without admitting she'd been hurt in the process. Chief would be furious.

But it wasn't Chief who first appeared at her side. Large, muscular arms scooped her up under her neck and knees as if she weighed nothing. She was pulled into a close embrace, surrounded by strong biceps and a rock-hard chest.

Ben.

He was like a fortress around her, shielding her from further harm. She removed her helmet and pressed her cheek to his chest, able to hear his rapid heartbeat even through his paramedic's jacket. She knew she should refuse his help, force herself to get down and walk on her own two feet, but she just couldn't bring herself to put up any resistance. For what might have been the first time in her life, Vee Bishop didn't fight her own need to be held.

Chapter Thirteen

Ben was quivering so much his teeth were chattering. Hopefully Vee couldn't tell how shaken up he was feeling. She'd been through enough without her seeing how much her daring rescue had affected him.

The thought that he might have lost her before he'd had the opportunity to tell her how he felt about her made him sick to his stomach. That even *he* hadn't known how he felt about her until she'd made the mad dash into the Salingers' home after Crystal was beside the point.

Crazy woman.

Wonderful, brave, and completely insane Vee Bishop. The lady who'd somehow slipped in and stolen his heart, and the woman he now knew he couldn't live without.

Ben had been walking in her direction when

Kent Salinger had broken for the house, and he'd watched in amazement as Vee had tackled him to the ground. To see a woman a little more than five feet tall take down a man who was well over six feet and a good hundred and eighty pounds was a sight in itself.

But then she'd run into the house herself to save the girl. Ben would have gone after her, except he didn't dare let go of Kent.

"Crazy woman," he muttered aloud as he strode back to the ambulance with Vee tucked safely in his arms.

Vee moaned. Ben wasn't sure whether that was in protest to what he'd said, or whether it was because she'd been injured in some way. There was blood all down the front of her jacket and a large, gaping cut on her chin.

One thing was for sure—she wasn't feeling 100 percent. Otherwise, she would have been all over him for saying that she was crazy.

"Almost there," he whispered, brushing his cheek against her hair. She reeked of smoke, but that didn't keep him from inhaling deeply. She was alive, and that was all that mattered. The smell of smoke was an acrid reminder to thank God that Vee was still here with him.

He wanted to blurt out how he felt about her, now that he'd finally figured it out himself. But he'd wait until she'd recovered a little bit before he blasted her with a whole new shock.

He reached the foot of the nearest fire truck just as she murmured, "Put me down, please."

Gingerly, he set her down on the ground, supporting her by the shoulders. "Are you able to sit?"

"Of course I can sit," she answered briskly, though her bold statement was interrupted by a coughing attack and she didn't immediately let go of his forearm.

"Easy does it. You're probably dizzy from all the smoke inhalation. Let me get you some oxygen and take care of that cut for you."

She protested, but he ignored her. Thankfully Zach had thought to leave a tank behind for Ben to use with Vee. With great care, he took her helmet from her tightly clenched fist and set it aside and then placed an oxygen mask over her mouth, careful to avoid the cut. He didn't think she'd need stitches, but he cleaned it up for her.

"Lady, don't *ever* do that to me again." His eyes met hers and his heart jammed in his throat. "You had me really worried there for a while."

"Crystal?" she choked out.

"She's good. She and her family are already on their way to Mercy Medical Center with Zach and Brody. She doesn't appear to have any external injuries, but they'll check her out to be certain and then treat her for smoke inhalation. They'll probably keep her overnight for observation, but thanks to you and your crazy stunt, that little girl is going to have a long and happy life."

"Zach and *Brody?*" she queried tremulously. "He's a cop. I don't understand. Why didn't you go with them in the ambulance? You know a lot more about medical issues than Brody does."

He leaned forward until his forehead was touching hers. "Are you kidding me? And leave you here without any support? Not in this lifetime. Besides, even a big lug like Brody can drive an ambulance. Don't worry. Zach is taking good care of Crystal."

Her eyes misted. One lone tear fell, but she quickly brushed it away with the back of her hand.

"My eyes are watering from all the smoke," she explained with a soft hiccup. Her voice was husky with emotion, but he imagined she would no doubt write that off to smoke inhalation, too.

He caressed her cheek with his palm and brushed a soft kiss against her forehead. "You did a very brave thing today, honey."

"She did a very *stupid* thing today." Chief Jenkins strode around the corner of the fire truck and glared down at Vee, his hands pressed against his hips. He was a formidable man on the best of occasions, but right now, with steam practically sizzling from his ears and his face streaked with black from the smoke, even Ben took a step back. "What were you thinking, Bishop?"

"Crystal," Vee answered weakly. "I had to save Emma's baby."

"You disobeyed a direct order! Not only that, but you didn't even use the common sense God gave you. You knew that house was about to come down around your ears. You, of all people, know how to assess structural damage in a fire. What you did was not only reckless, but it put your fellow firefighters at risk trying to help you. You're suspended from active duty until further notice."

Vee shook her head as if she didn't quite understand Chief's words to her. Her eyes were misty again, and Ben thought she might break into tears at any moment.

Vee Bishop. Crying.

Clearly the poor woman was in shock. Ben stepped forward, blocking Chief's view of Vee.

"Look here, Chief," he started. Ben ignored the fact that Chief had turned his dominating glare upon him. Better that than for him to continue hovering over Vee.

He reached for Chief's elbow and pulled him

aside. "Now, I know Vee disobeyed a direct order," he started.

"Yes, she did," Chief barked. "And don't try to talk me out of suspending her. She knew the consequences when she made the decision to run into that house on her own."

"But she did save the girl." He was stating the obvious, but that had to count for something, didn't it?

"That's irrelevant. People in our line of work have to obey orders, keep the chain of command. Otherwise you've got utter chaos."

"I know," Ben agreed. "But don't you think you can give her a bit of a break right now?" He leaned toward Chief and lowered his voice. "I think she's in shock. She needs medical attention. I *know* she inhaled a lot of smoke in there, and I haven't really been able to assess her for external wounds. Kent Salinger gave her a good clip on the chin with the heel of his boot."

Chief adjusted his helmet, drawing it lower over his brow. After a moment, he nodded.

"Do what you have to, Atwood. See that she's properly cared for. We'll deal with this later."

"Yes, sir."

"And you," Chief said, stepping around Ben to hover over Vee and point an accusatory finger at her, "promise me you won't do anything else foolish until we have ourselves a little talk back at the station tomorrow."

"Yes, sir," Vee replied weakly.

"Make no mistake about it. We *will* have that talk," he promised. "Don't you go thinking you're out of the woods yet, Bishop."

"Yes, sir," Vee said again, then sighed heavily and sank back on her shoulders.

"Are we good, Chief?" Ben queried, squatting down beside Vee to support her shoulders. He brushed a tendril of hair from her forehead that had escaped the knot at the back of her neck.

"Take care of our girl," Chief said and then turned on his heels and marched away, shaking his head as he went.

That was exactly what he planned to do. Not just now, but for as long as Vee would let him.

"Take it easy there, honey," he murmured, shifting on his knees so he was cradling her in his arms. "Don't worry about Chief Jenkins. He's just a little overwrought from trying to fight the fire—and from nearly losing Crystal Salinger and the best firefighter in his unit. He'll come off his high horse once things have settled down around here."

Vee squeezed her eyes closed and pinched her lips together. "You heard him. I'm suspended from the department."

"We'll see," he murmured.

Not on his watch. He'd find some way to keep Vee from the repercussions of her actions if he had to band the entire fire department behind her to do so. Chief couldn't fight everyone. And anyway, Ben guessed that Chief Jenkins wouldn't be quite so angry once he'd had the opportunity to cool off.

He sat silently with her for a moment, reveling in the fact that she was in his arms. Even with her hair unkempt from the helmet and her face smudged with smoke, she was the most beautiful woman he'd ever known.

His heart swelled and closed up his throat when she leaned backward and their gazes met. She didn't say a word, but her glinting eyes spoke volumes.

Gratitude. Tenderness. And…something more? Or was he just imagining what he wanted to see there?

The world around them might as well not have existed at all. He was keenly aware of Vee—the way she looked, the way she smelled, the way she sounded as her breathing increased through the oxygen mask. None of it should have been the least bit romantic, but Ben wouldn't choose to be anywhere else but here with Vee in his arms.

He desperately wanted to kiss her again, to

discover once and for all if the emotions he was reading in her eyes were real or just a figment of his overactive imagination, his deep desire that she reciprocate his own feelings. This time, she would have no doubt of his intentions.

This time *he* had no doubt of his intentions.

As if reading his mind, she twisted in his arms, tilting her head toward his. He reached around to the nape of her neck and slid his fingers over the elastic that kept the oxygen mask attached. Carefully, oh so slowly, he loosened the mask and slipped it over her head.

"Vee, I—" he began, his voice in a low timbre he didn't recognize.

She stopped him with a finger to his lips. She shook her head and then ran her palm across his cheek and behind his neck, pulling him closer, tilting her mouth up to his.

So there was no need to say the words, after all. She felt as he did, that they should be together.

Vee was his. He had only to prove it with a kiss.

He tilted his head, taking his sweet, sweet time, his mouth hovering over hers until he heard her gasp in anticipation. Her warm breath mixed with his, intoxicating him.

His gaze flicked away for just one second, but it was enough to change his world. His eyes alighted on her helmet, forgotten for the moment and tipped upside down. Her name was written inside, in bold, permanent black ink marker.

Veronica Jayne Bishop.

Chapter Fourteen

Knife, meet heart.

Broken trust was a sharp weapon, and it hit Ben right in the chest, its ragged edges cutting deeply.

He scrambled backward, jumping to his feet, nearly knocking Vee—*Veronica Jayne*—over in the process.

"Wha—?" she mumbled incoherently, her eyes heavily lidded and her full lips half-pursed, poised for a kiss.

The initial pain and shock Ben felt at seeing her name turned to humiliation and then anger in a matter of seconds, rolling from one emotion to another like a snowball gaining both strength and momentum as it spun down a hill.

"I'll bet you and your friends had a good laugh at my expense, didn't you?" he bit out, spinning on his heels so that he didn't have to look at her.

"I don't know what you mean." She sounded perplexed and bewildered and a little hurt herself.

Like she had any right to be.

"How could you?"

"How could I what?"

"Don't play dumb with me, *Veronica Jayne*."

"What did you just call me?"

"Veronica Jayne. That's your name, isn't it?"

"Well, yes, but—"

"You must really think I'm an idiot."

"No, Ben. I never once, not even for a moment, thought that you were an idiot."

"And yet I played your little game. I told you all my deepest secrets so that you could make fun of me with your friends."

"I never laughed at you." Now she sounded angry.

Angry? What right did she have to be angry? That was *his* emotion.

"I didn't know."

Really? She was going to try to *lie* her way out of this now? He narrowed his eyes on her and tilted his head, daring her to continue.

She blinked several times and her gaze dropped away. How much more obvious could she be?

Guilty as charged.

"I really didn't know, Ben," she continued,

her voice cracking under the strain of speaking. "I only found out just moments before the call for the fire came in."

"What does that matter?" he snapped. "You should have told me right away. You should have told me as soon as you found out."

He wasn't at all convinced she was telling him the truth about when she'd discovered he was the BJ she'd been emailing. It was gut-wrenching even to consider that she might have known all along. That she had played him like a puppet, making him into a fool.

He certainly felt like a fool.

And even if she hadn't known, as she was claiming, she still should have come forward the moment she'd discovered the truth. But Vee Bishop apparently didn't care for the truth. And anyway, he'd known all along that she didn't care for him. Whatever grudge she held against him, she'd paid him back for it—with interest.

"I can't believe I fell for you. F-fell for your ruse," he stammered, correcting himself. "Well, I have got news for you."

He turned back to her, crouching down and tilting his head so their lips were as close as they had been in the moments before he'd seen the name in her helmet.

She sat frozen to the spot. He couldn't even feel her breath this time, but he knew his own was quick and ragged, and his heart was pumping overtime. There was only one thing left for him to say.

"Game over."

Vee folded the last of her shirts and tucked them into the suitcase lying open on her bed. That was it, then. Everything she needed to leave Serendipity behind.

And with it, her heart.

She couldn't believe that she could get this close to happiness and then have it be ripped out from underneath her. Every time she closed her eyes, she remembered Ben—his forehead touching hers, how strong his arms were around her, the warmth and anticipation of his lips hovering over hers.

The fury that scorched his face when he had learned the truth about her.

And what could she say? She *had* known that Ben was BJ. That she'd found out only moments before the emergency had been called seemed irrelevant. Ben would never have listened to any rationale she might have given for not coming clean with the shocking news.

He was convinced she'd betrayed him.

And wasn't that partially her fault, too? No, she hadn't deliberately deceived him, but she'd spent years holding on to a grudge, refusing to follow God's commandment to forgive. After the way she'd treated him for so long, could she blame him for thinking she'd play this kind of cruel trick on him?

She moved to her sock drawer and scooped the entire contents of the drawer into her arms and then tossed them haphazardly into the suitcase, using the socks to fill the nooks and crevices of her suitcase.

Oh, Ben. They *knew* each other, both as Ben and Vee and as BJ and Veronica Jayne. They'd shared their thoughts, their feelings, their deepest hopes and dreams through their email letters. They'd shared a kiss as Ben and Vee—and she'd thought, in that moment before he'd seen her full name on her helmet, that there would be more than just one simple kiss between them, that she'd read a lifetime in his bronze-green eyes.

She'd believed the unbelievable. And how stupid was that?

She was in love with Ben Atwood. If Ben was BJ, all the better, right? And she was Veronica Jayne. That should be a good thing. Inside her heart, she really was that person—the one he'd said he cared for. The one he'd encouraged in the Lord more times than she could count.

And now—thanks to one big, tangled misunderstanding—it was all ruined.

She had to look toward the future—toward the Sacred Heart Mission, where she'd be out of Serendipity and out of Ben's life. He'd never leave her heart or her mind, but hopefully her leaving would make things easier on him.

That was the least she could do, with the mess she had made of both of their lives.

"Are you out of your mind?" Zach spotted Ben while he did bench presses—two hundred pounds. Benching the heavy weight was getting easier. His life was a blooming disaster and it didn't look like it was going to get better any-time soon, but all the angst had done wonders for his workout routine.

Not that that was any comfort to his heart. How was he going to live without Vee?

"I've been benching two hundred for a while now. It's no big deal."

"I wasn't talking about the weights. I was talking about the woman. You are seriously just going to let her walk out of your life?"

"She isn't going anywhere that I know of. At least not at the moment."

Their Spanish project was finished, on his side, at least. Just this morning, he'd emailed her the final presentation for her to accept or reject, as she pleased. He was done with it.

And then, who knew? Eventually, she was headed for stateside mission work.

What would happen to the plans they'd been making? He sighed inwardly. It would be best for all involved if he scrapped the whole thing—started over and applied for a completely different mission. Working alongside Vee would be pure torture for him now.

"So what are you waiting for?" Zach prodded, taking the bar from him and placing it in the rack. "Until you can bench two-fifty?"

"I'm not waiting for anything. I'm done with it."

"Then you're an idiot."

"Thank you very much," Ben said with more than a little bitterness in his voice. "I think we've already clearly established that point. I was played, and I fell for it." His flower girl. Having difficulty finding herself. Letting her hair down. The clues were all there, and he hadn't seen them. How stupid could he be?

"Fell for *her,* you mean."

"Whatever."

"So, I repeat, what are you going to do about it? How long is it going to take you to admit that you need her in your life and you're willing to forgive her for whatever it is that you think she's done to you?"

"What do you mean, what I *think* she's done to me?"

"I mean you haven't really given her the benefit of the doubt, and I think she deserves at least that much. From what you've told me, she said that she only learned it was you right before we got called away for the emergency. She wouldn't have had time to digest the shock, much less figure out a way to tell you anything."

Ben grunted and rolled to a sitting position. He didn't want to admit that his partner might have a valid point.

"What if the roles were reversed? What if she'd been the one to send her picture to you?"

"So what if she had? I would have spoken up right away and let her know I was BJ."

"Would you really? Because if it were me, I would have been reeling from the shock of finding out. Of all the women in the whole wide world, of all the places she could be living, she's right here in Serendipity with you—and not only that, but you guys even work at the same fire station together."

"What are the odds?"

"Exactly. Which is why I think Vee deserves a chance. She's a good woman, Ben, and I think deep down in your heart you know it. You have to admit, you've had your share of dating disasters. But maybe this is why none of those women worked out—so you'd be free when the right one came along. I can't think of a better person for you to end up with."

Ben moved to the free weights and started his biceps curls, not even bothering to keep a count in his head.

"Stop meddling," he protested in a low voice.

"Okay, I'll shut up. But consider this. You really liked Veronica Jayne. You and she seemed like really close friends. You understood each other. You had the same goals and ambitions and dreams. Friendship is really important in a relationship, take it from me."

"Apparently I *am* taking it from you," he growled.

"I'm not finished. So on one hand you have Veronica Jayne, and then on the other hand there is Vee—you two have sparks flying so high that the fire department would have a hard time containing you."

That much was true, which was why Ben thought it was a good idea to stay as far away from Vee as possible. He wasn't sure he was going to be able to keep his resolve once their eyes met or he saw her beautiful smile.

"What I'm saying is this—Vee and Veronica Jayne are one in the same person. How much more of a blessing are you looking for, buddy?"

Ben felt like he'd been flash-frozen. He dropped the weights to his side and stared open-mouthed at Zach.

"She made a mistake—fine. Is it really unforgivable? Is holding on to your grudge worth losing your chance of being happy? You love her, you dolt. So go get her, and stop being so stubborn."

Zach was right. What was he doing lifting weights with a sweaty guy friend when he could be in the company of Vee—Veronica Jayne?

He hadn't given her the benefit of the doubt. Trust went both ways. He'd been so shocked by the revelation that Vee was Veronica Jayne that he hadn't given her a chance to explain. She was probably as stunned as he was by the discovery. Maybe she should have told him, but like Zach said, it was a mistake. He'd made plenty of his own.

Letting her go would be the biggest mistake of all.

He had to find her. Now.

"I'm out of here," Ben said, wiping the sweat off his forehead with the towel draped around his neck.

Zach laughed. "It's about time."

Ben quickly showered and dressed and headed straight for Emerson's Hardware. It was early in the day, but he hoped he'd be able to catch Vee alone so he'd be able to talk to her and clear up this whole mess once and for all.

As he walked, he tried phoning her cell, but she wouldn't pick up. She'd probably blocked his number. She obviously didn't want to talk to him—not that he could blame her after the way he'd reacted.

That only strengthened his resolve to make things right. And then he would kiss Vee senseless and prove to her once and for all that as Ben and as BJ, as Vee and Veronica Jayne, he was in love with her.

When he got to Emerson's, he went straight to the gardening department, but she wasn't there, so he asked for her at the front desk.

She'd *quit* Emerson's Hardware just the day before. The news struck him mute. No two weeks' notice. No explanations about where she was going or why she had decided to up and resign so suddenly. Just an apology and a farewell.

She was leaving.

A dark pit grew in the center of his stomach and filled with raw dread. Vee couldn't leave. Or more accurately, she couldn't leave *him,* though he'd certainly given her no reason to stay.

He jogged as fast as his legs would carry him

over to her apartment. He had to catch her before she left for good.

But he ran into a dead end there, too. Her rent had been paid until the end of the month, and her apartment had been emptied. No forwarding address. No hints as to where she might have gone.

He was winded and his heart was pumping overtime, but that didn't stop him from making a sprint for Vee's father's house. Surely she would stop in there to say goodbye. And if she wasn't there, she would have to have told her father where she was going or at least how to get in touch with her.

"I'm sorry, son," her father said when he opened the door to Ben. "Vee only told me she'd be in touch after she was settled. I wish I could tell you more. Here, though—she left you this note. Maybe that has a clue to where she is."

Ben took the folded piece of lined notebook paper and opened it, holding his breath as he scanned the contents. It was short and to the point, with beautiful, measured handwriting that for some reason reminded him of the emails he shared with Veronica Jayne.

Dear Ben,
I know that nothing I can say will change
what happened, but I want you to know

*how truly sorry I am for the way things
went down.*

*Since I don't know whether you will even
speak to me or not, I'm leaving you this
letter, which in a way seems oddly appropriate. I want to let you know that nothing
that happened between us was make-be-
lieve. What I felt for you—feel for you—is
and will always be real.*

*For what it's worth, I really care about
you.*
Love,
Vee

Stunned, Ben left Vee's father's house and
walked aimlessly, eventually finding himself
in the park. He slumped onto a bench and held
his head in his hands.

What was he going to do now? She evidently
hadn't told a solitary soul where she was going.
She was running away, not only from him, but
from everything she knew and loved.

There was no question that he would go after
her. He just had to figure out where she'd gone.
It wasn't going to be easy. But then memories
flashed through his head of long conversations
via email of plans for the future.

Maybe finding her was going to be the sim-
plest thing in the world.

Chapter Fifteen

Vee sat at a desk in the far end of the class-room, staring out the window, watching children running around on a playground. They all seemed so energetic. So innocent. So care-free. So happy.

She sighed. She should be examining her syllabus for the class ahead. The introductory training manual for the Sacred Heart Mission was enormous. It was a week-long class, and Vee imagined it would be quite demanding.

She'd been through the fire academy, so she wasn't too worried about mastering the material, but she needed to keep her mind where it belonged—here at the mission and not home in Serendipity, where Ben was probably at the station, kicking back with Zach and the other guys, eating his *secret* chili and not giving her a single thought at all.

The mission teacher moved to the front of the room and started writing his lecture notes on the whiteboard. Vee closed her eyes. This ought to be one of the most exciting moments of her life—beginning the training she'd waited for years to do.

She had to cling to that—the external goals she'd set. The calling she felt from God to help other people. She had to do something, and this was it. She opened her eyes, determined to make this work despite how her heart ached.

She had read the first paragraph of her syllabus when there was a noise at the door on the other side of the room.

"Excuse me. Pardon me. I'm sorry. I guess I'm late."

Suddenly, it was as if the atmosphere grew warmer. More humid, making it hard to breathe. Vee's heart leapt into her throat at the same time she tried to sweep in a breath, and the result was audible.

She would know that deep, rich voice anywhere.

She glanced across the room, unwilling to believe what her ears were telling her.

Ben was there—with his dark curly hair and his luminous green-bronze eyes and his biceps so huge they were straining through his black T-shirt.

Their eyes met and locked. Her world tipped, turning sideways on its axis and making her head rush in a dizzy loop while her heart pounded maddeningly in her chest.

What was he doing here?

Ben—her BJ—was the most handsome man she'd ever laid eyes on, better even than she could have imagined.

His eyes glimmered as he smiled his charming half smile, and she was certain every woman in the room grew just a little bit giddy. Somehow she knew, though, that his smile was only for her.

"Ben," she choked out as he strode across the room, not even bothering to excuse himself when he bumped a couple of desks.

"Vee." That was all he said before he framed her face and kissed her. This time there was no doubt of his feelings. He was pouring out all his emotions right here in front of everyone.

And Vee wanted to be nowhere else in the world but in his arms.

"Vee," he repeated, kissing her once again for emphasis. "You left without saying goodbye."

"I didn't think you'd want to hear it from me."

"I don't."

She frowned, confused. "Then why are you here?"

"I don't want you to say goodbye, Vee. Ever.

We can both stay here and complete our introductory courses for the Sacred Heart Mission, but first I have something to say. I love you. Will you marry me?"

Vee would have suspected that she'd heard wrong had the entire class not broken out shouting and clapping. There was no mistaking that.

But the sound faded as her eyes met Ben's and she read the love shining in his gaze. He meant it. He wanted to marry her—Veronica Jayne Bishop, for all she was both on the inside and the outside. He knew her—everything about her, just as she knew about him. And she felt the same way.

"Vee, honey?" Ben said with a nervous chuckle. "You're kind of leaving me hanging here."

Vee laughed along with him, her joy bubbling over. "Of course I'll marry you, Ben, or BJ, or whatever your name is today. I've been waiting for quite some time to tell you that I love you with my whole heart."

Ben whooped and pulled her into his arms, kissing her again, more fervently this time. He kept repeating the same line between kisses.

"I love you. I love you. I love you."

Vee couldn't hear those words enough.

"Um, excuse me," came a deep voice from the front of the room.

Ben and Vee turned as one, without letting go of each other.

It was the teacher who'd spoken. He had a wry smile on his face. "We're all really happy for you, and congratulations are definitely in order."

"Thank you, sir," Ben responded.

"However," the teacher continued, "do you think you could continue this happy reunion later, after my class is finished?"

Ben and Vee laughed and slid into adjoining chairs, his warm fingers still clasping hers across the aisle. It was then that Vee knew they would never be parted again.

* * * * *

Dear Reader,

Thank you for joining me for another heartfelt romantic adventure in Serendipity, Texas. If you happened to have missed the prior books in the Email Order Brides series, the titles are *Phoebe's Groom, The Doctor's Secret Son* and *The Nanny's Twin Blessings.* You can find these books and many others of my backlist available for order from online booksellers in both print and ebook format.

In *Meeting Mr. Right,* both Vee and Ben struggled with their identities as adults because of traumatic bullying instances in their childhoods. Our past is so firmly etched into our hearts that sometimes it's hard to let go and learn to live in the present. But unless we focus on what's going on around us in our day-to-day lives, we're going to miss out on many opportunities to see God working in our lives and to discover new occasions to love and serve one another.

I hope you've been encouraged by Ben and Vee's story and that it's been a blessing to you. My thoughts and prayers are always with the readers of my stories, and hearing from you is a great treasure to me. Please email me at debkastnerbooks@gmail.com or leave a comment on my fan page on Facebook. I'm also on Twitter (@debkastner). Hope to see you online soon!

Keep the faith,

Deb Kastner

Questions for Discussion

1. At the beginning of the novel, Vee is suspicious of Ben's behavior. Why? Do you think she's right to be suspicious?

2. Both Ben and Vee had trauma in their childhoods that influenced the people they became as adults. How have the events in your childhood affected the person you are today?

3. Ben and Vee were tormented by bullies in their younger years. Do you think bullying is still a problem in today's schools? How can we work toward a better experience for all of today's schoolchildren?

4. What are the major themes running throughout this book? Which are important to you, and why?

5. Vee tried not to care for Ben, but she couldn't seem to help herself. What character traits did Ben possess that appealed to her despite her initial misgivings?

6. If you could meet one character in this book, who would it be? Why?

7. Vee's best friend Olivia forgave Ben for the way he'd burned her in their relationship, yet for most of the novel, Vee seems unable to do so. Why do you think that is?

8. In chapter seven, when Ben becomes personally affected by Vee's dress-and-heels transformation, he begins to doubt his own ability to look beyond outward appearances. Was there ever a time you judged someone by their outward appearance only to ultimately discover you were wrong about them?

9. Discuss the meaning of the following scripture verses as they relate to the novel: *As in water face reflects face, so a man's heart reveals the man.* Proverbs 27:19 and *For the Lord does not see as man sees; for man looks at the outward appearance, but the Lord looks at the heart.* I Samuel 16:7.

10. At what point in the novel do you think Vee started to soften toward Ben?

11. What do you think Vee should have done when she discovered that her online friend BJ was actually Ben Atwood if the fire had not happened directly afterward?

12. Why do you think Ben believed Vee had been intentionally deceiving him? How would you have felt in his circumstances?

13. How do you think Vee felt when Ben accused her of viciously and deliberately misleading him?

14. Both Ben and Vee receive wise counseling from their friends at different points in the novel. Relate a situation in which God has used a friend to help guide you to a good decision.

15. What is the takeaway value of this book? What will you remember the most?

LARGER-PRINT BOOKS!

GET 2 FREE LARGER-PRINT NOVELS PLUS 2 FREE MYSTERY GIFTS

Love Inspired

Larger-print novels are now available...

LILPDIR13

Love Inspired®
SUSPENSE
RIVETING INSPIRATIONAL ROMANCE

Watch for our series of edge-
of-your-seat suspense novels.
These contemporary tales
of intrigue and romance
feature Christian characters
facing challenges to their faith...
and their lives!

AVAILABLE IN REGULAR
& LARGER-PRINT FORMATS

For exciting stories that reflect traditional values,
visit:
www.ReaderService.com

LISUSDIR11B